IT STARTED WITH A KISS

Gardening TV sex symbol Rory Oakhurst has a vacancy on his team and TV journalist Annabel Grainger gets the job. However, she is devastated to learn that Rory considers her selection to have been influenced by her privileged background. Despite this, a grudging attraction grows between them. Then Annabel overhears a conversation which makes her think someone is plotting to cause Rory's downfall. But will he trust her enough to allow her through his barricade of toughness?

BETH JAMES

IT STARTED
WITH A KISS

Complete and Unabridged

LINFORD
Leicester

First published in Great Britain in 2005

First Linford Edition
published 2006

British Library CIP Data

James, Beth
  It started with a kiss.—Large print ed.—
Linford romance library
1. Television programs—Fiction
2. Gardening—Fiction
3. Love stories
4. Large type books
I. Title
823.9'2 [F]

ISBN 1–84617–451–1

Published by
F. A. Thorpe (Publishing)
Anstey, Leicestershire

Set by Words & Graphics Ltd.
Anstey, Leicestershire
Printed and bound in Great Britain by
T. J. International Ltd., Padstow, Cornwall

1

'Of course this whole interview thing is a farce. A set-up. Miss I've-got-a-rich-powerful-daddy gets the job.'

Hardly able to believe she was hearing correctly, Annabel paused outside the door, her hand suspended in mid air. She recognised the slight Scots lilt in the voice and knew it had to belong to her main interviewer. Her feeling of confidence and well-being was slaughtered at a stroke, but catching her full lower lip between her teeth, she waited until the murmuring at the other side of the door had lowered enough so as to be inaudible, then counted to ten, took a deep breath and knocked.

'Come in,' the terse command came.

There were two men seated behind the desk. One was in his fifties wearing a collar and tie, neat and efficient looking, every inch a businessman. His companion was in his early thirties with hazel-coloured hair that, though clean, appeared not to have seen a comb for some time. He had a jutting nose, brooding eyes, which were at the moment surveying her as though she might be carrying an infectious disease. His creased, casual clothing could have come from the nearest charity shop. Rory Oakhurst, for Annabel recognised him straight away, looked exactly as he looked on the television, anything but businesslike.

'Hi!' Rory said as he got to his feet and stretched out a hand that, when Annabel put hers into it, somehow didn't feel welcoming.

He smiled briefly, showing a set of very white slightly-crooked teeth. Annabel caught her breath. His smile up close was even more devastating than on the screen.

'Hello,' she replied trying not to wince from his brief handshake. 'I'm Annabel. Annabel Grainger.'

But he knew that already, she thought to herself. He knew all about her, or obviously thought he did. After all, hadn't he just described her as being Little Miss I've-got-a-rich-powerful-daddy?

Remembering that and seething inwardly, she allowed herself to be introduced to Peter Fielding, the TV executive representing Sebastian Melrose, the programme producer and seated herself opposite the two men.

Rory studied the paperwork in front of him then treated her to a penetrating stare.

'Well, you've made a good start in children's television. I watched one of your shows. There's no doubt you've got what it takes to be an excellent presenter.'

Annabel waited for the 'but' she knew was coming.

'However,' Rory went on, 'this job is a little different. It is not a cosy studio job. It's an out-in-all weathers, do that take fifteen times if necessary, get dirty, work physically to the point of exhaustion, that kind of job.'

Annabel smiled.

'I'm aware of the nature of the job,' she said quietly. 'That's one of the reasons I applied.'

Another penetrating glare, but Annabel stared back, smiling calmly, although she was anything but calm inside. No, inside, her stomach was churning with a mixture of anger, fear and something else she couldn't quite explain.

Rory looked irritated.

'So if you break a finger nail or your mascara gets smudged, I don't expect tears and hysterics, right?'

Annabel smiled again. She'd discovered she quite liked irritating him.

'Of course not,' she said serenely, 'anymore than you would throw a tantrum if your autocue got stuck or your co-presenter fluffed their lines.'

She paused but her smile never faltered.

'If you look at my references you'll see I've always tried to behave professionally no matter what the circumstances.'

Got you, she thought as Rory

narrowed his eyes and leaned back in his chair. Rory Oakhurst was well-known for being unable to suffer fools gladly and his occasional bouts of temper on set were legendary.

Peter Fielding cleared his throat.

'There are a few things I'd like to go through with you, Annabel,' he said, 'and don't take Rory's interviewing techniques too seriously. We all know his bark is worse than his bite.'

Annabel smiled again although, looking at Rory's mutinous expression, she privately thought the opposite to be true.

★   ★   ★

'Well, Anna, how did it go?'

Annabel held the phone close to her ear and wrinkled her nose.

'Not sure really. Dad, you didn't have anything to do with getting me on the short list, did you?'

There was an imperceptible pause.

'Of course not, darling. Ran into

5

Sebastian by accident, just mentioned you were up for it and I had every faith that you would do well. Why you're so keen to do it, I don't pretend to understand, after all it's not a very feminine occupation, wallowing around in mud, but I know you, Anna, and you always give everything your best shot.'

Try telling Mr Rory Oakhurst that, Annabel thought.

After chatting for a few more moments to her father, who was on his way to a meeting, Annabel laid down the phone and tried to put the image of Rory Oakhurst out of her mind. An hour later, having changed TV channels half a dozen times, she admitted to herself that she was failing miserably.

For about the fifteenth time, she wondered what he had thought of her. It had not been what she would call a relaxed interview. He'd been very cagey throughout, occasionally shooting her penetrating questions about her gardening background which, unfortunately, was not anywhere near so deep or

6

experienced as his. On the personal side, he'd asked what her commitments were, as sometimes she might be required to work later than expected due to a technical glitch or weather conditions.

Annabel had explained that she was a free agent and intent on building a successful career, a few hours overtime and bad weather would be no problem.

'Hmm,' Rory said. 'You may be called upon to go to the other side of the country or even abroad at short notice. How would you feel about that?'

His grey eyes gleamed at her from under his tousled hair.

'Excited,' Annabel said.

For a second, there had been a certain frisson between them, a spark of recognition. Then, breaking the spell, Rory had looked back at his notes and Peter had taken over the interview once again.

'Sebastian Melrose is our producer, as you know,' he said. 'He's quite impressed with your record so far, so I think it's safe for you to assume you're a serious contender.'

Remembering that now, Annabel sighed. She hoped so much she would get the job. She loved gardening, she loved garden design. She knew the names, common and Latin, of every plant and flower in her father's extensive garden in Gloucestershire.

OK, so her knowledge of fruit and vegetables was not so good and she sometimes got confused with the many different tree families, but on the whole her knowledge was excellent and her television experience had been proven. So why shouldn't she get the job?

It just wasn't fair of Rory to assume that she'd made the short list on anything other than merit. All right, she was willing to admit her father was rich and powerful. He had a seat on the board of half a dozen successful companies, and he knew a lot of influential people. But that didn't mean that he pulled strings for her, or that she hadn't had to work really hard to become successful in her own field of television journalism.

She'd come out of university the same as her contemporaries — keen, fresh, eager to learn and, yes, she'd been lucky a couple of times, been in the right place at the right time.

At the last minute, she'd been called on to take over when a well-known presenter was suddenly rushed to hospital with appendicitis. That had been the break that had made her, because Annabel possessed the rare ability to appear calm and unfazed, even while feeling nauseous and panic-stricken inside.

She had picked up the microphone and, taking directions through her earpiece, conducted live interviews on an emotive subject as though she'd had weeks of preparations. When the camera had stopped rolling, there had been a round of applause from the technicians and her colleagues alike. She'd been proud of herself that day, had known that she was doing a job she loved and was good at it and that she'd earned that respect with no help from her father.

Thinking of Richard Grainger now, a small frown appeared between Annabel's brows. How could you be cross with your father for loving you too much? Maybe he loved her so much because her mother had died tragically young and he felt he had to make up for all the mother love she missed out on.

Annabel had always thought this to be the case and tried not to appear ungrateful that her father attempted infallibly to smooth life's obstacles out of her way. Well, there was only so much any father could do.

Annabel smiled wryly as, completely uninvited, an image of Rory's attractive, square-jawed face appeared before her. She had the feeling that Rory Oakhurst would be one obstacle even Richard Grainger would be unable to shift.

★ ★ ★

Rory Oakhurst scowled into his pint glass and drummed his fingers on the table top next to it. He was sitting alone in an unfashionable pub in an unfashionable part of London. It was a pub where, although he was recognised, he could drink undisturbed, and right now he needed some undisturbed thinking time, because he knew, he just knew Annabel Grainger was going to be trouble.

For a start, why was it necessary to rope in another woman? After a slow beginning **Dig Your Garden** had shot up the ratings chart. They'd started out small with Rory as front man leading the way, doing most of the physical work himself with occasional help from trainee, Andy. Emma had been added to the team purely in order to ask inane questions, a move suggested by Sebastian Melrose, the producer, which Rory argued initially would be a huge mistake but discovered was in fact the very catalyst that made the programme so successful.

At first, he'd thought the ladies in the audience would feel patronised that they were represented by a young girl who knew so little, but he'd reckoned without the female psyche. It appeared that Emma very often asked the questions they were itching to ask themselves and, in a way that was amusing. Before long, between them, Rory, Andy and Emma had made gardening not only interesting but fun.

Yes, Sebastian had been right on that occasion and that was why Rory, after a token argument, had eventually capitulated and agreed to another woman, this time an interviewer with a view to becoming co-presenter. She had to be pretty, Sebastian stated, pretty and a professional presenter. Why, Rory had argued. He didn't care what she looked like, as long as she knew what she was talking about, after all, she was going to have to answer questions, too.

So he'd looked down the list of names and saw Zoe Blackstop among the hopefuls and felt a moment's optimism. Zoe was basically a gardener's gardener — dirt under the nails, mud-splattered jeans, an attractive smile and an encyclopaedia knowledge of plants. With a horticultural college background and a couple of years' experience in the extensive gardens of one of the most well-known stately homes in the south east, she must surely be the prime candidate.

Not only that, but Rory had interviewed her on television himself and knew that he liked her, and that she had an easy, natural manner that went well with his own, slightly more intense personality. He had also picked up on the fact that she came from a poor, working-class background but was very, very ambitious. Being hungry for success was something that Rory could relate to more than most. He knew that Zoe would work her socks off and not much would stop her until she'd struggled to the top of the heap. He would have liked to help her in that struggle.

However, Sebastian had other ideas. There, at the top of the short list, was the name Annabel Grainger.

'I take your point about Zoe. I may keep Zoe in mind for another project,' Sebastian had said thoughtfully. 'But Annabel's the one. She's the one we want. We've got the female audience tied up. They've all got the hots for you, Rory. Now we need to catch the fellows, the young ones, too, and this baby, she's got what it takes.'

Thinking of this now, Rory squirmed. The thought of his female audience panting with lust every time he flexed his biceps was not attractive to him and the prospect of Annabel and himself appearing together as some kind of double act was even less so. But as Sebastian said, it was not only gardening, it was entertainment and the competition was fierce.

Rory knew he couldn't afford to flout Sebastian and do his own thing or before he knew it he'd be back to running his garden centre, which although satisfying wasn't as satisfying as presenting **Dig Your Garden**.

Of course, he hadn't given in without a fight. He'd praised Zoe to the sky, insisted that Sebastian watch the interview she'd done with him on an earlier programme, but no, Sebastian was adamant.

'Hold Zoe in reserve if you like,' Sebastian agreed finally. 'As I said, I'm keeping her in mind myself for another idea I've been toying with. But the public already knows Annabel and they like her. Her main job will be to take the interviews you can't get to. You know the ones up in the wilds of Scotland and, don't glower at me Rory, parts of your beloved Scotland can be so wild they're positively furious.'

He paused for a moment as though he'd said something very amusing.

'Also, even you have to admit that in the looks department Annabel wins hands down. Anyway I owe her dad a favour.'

The last remark had been the one that really set Rory's teeth on edge. Old school tie stuff again. How he hated it, but he had gone to the interview with bad grace, despising himself for being resigned to the outcome, and then the door had opened, Annabel walked in and, well, he hadn't stopped reeling since. Pretty was the understatement of the year. He'd seen a tape of one of her children's shows recorded a couple of years previously, and admitted to himself that she was easy on the eye, but he'd still been unprepared for the reality, unprepared for the softness of her skin, the silkiness of her blonde hair, the blueness or steadiness of her gaze, the melody in her low-speaking voice and the indefinable something that made his heart lurch.

Rory gripped hard on the handle of his pint glass. She needn't think she was going to get any favours from him, just because she was pretty — well, beautiful actually. She needn't think she was going to be allowed hours in the ladies renewing her make-up. She'd looked smart as paint in her businesslike pin-striped suit with just the suggestion of a frilly blouse at her cleavage.

Perhaps, when she realised that comfort and warmth was more the order of dressing than designer labels, she'd also recognise it wasn't all sniffing pretty flowers and flirting with the camera. She'd said she'd always been interested in gardening, that what she didn't know she was willing to learn. Well, she was going to learn just how hard it really was.

Rory took another sip of beer. He hadn't been able to just walk into his job, he'd had to earn it. He'd had to do it the hard way. No rich daddy, no university education, just a Saturday job in the open air, then agricultural college and a job with the National Trust. Rory knew all about hard work and before he'd finished with her so would Miss Pretty-I-can-do-anything-because-daddy-says-so. She might be able to wind Daddy and Sebastian and half the male population of the UK round her little finger, but he wouldn't be one of their number, no way!

A shadow passed over Rory's dark features. Funny that Sebastian had been so keen to employ Annabel. For a moment he wondered if there was a bit more to if than that, if maybe his interest in Annabel was more than simply professional and all this 'I owe her Dad a favour' stuff was a blind. Politics were not Rory's strong suit. His straight talking had got him into trouble more than once in the past, but now he was at least able to recognise that people at the top, such as Sebastian, often had a different way of working and a whole separate agenda.

He was also wise enough to know what from the outset the two of them were much too unalike ever to really warm to one another. But maybe Annabel had warmed to Sebastian. Maybe there was a great big bonfire going on between them. Something about that idea didn't appeal so he quickly put it out of his mind and went back to wondering just how it was that Sebastian and he had managed not to have a major fall-out.

He supposed it was mainly because they didn't see one another too often, and because, despite their differences, they'd developed a mutual respect for one another's work that they had worked together well so far. There was often a calculating expression in Sebastian's narrow dark eyes that Rory didn't quite trust, and a stillness about him which he found almost sinister on occasions. Rory was always aware that Sebastian, with a string of successes behind him, was very experienced in television production. Sebastian was all powerful. Sebastian was possibly dangerous. But it was Sebastian who called the tune.

So, a phone conference between the two men after the interview had resulted in an agreement that Annabel was to be given a settling-in period working on the show at ground roots level. Rory had laughed politely at the pun. If the audience liked her, a series of interviews with famous gardeners in some of the country's most beautiful gardens would follow.

Although eventually reduced to five minutes' air time, the interviews would be a very important part of the programme. Thinking about it, he sighed. Now Rory had met Annabel, he knew Sebastian had been right, whatever his own interests were. If her gardening knowledge was up to it, with her confidence and background, she'd be perfect for the job.

But it didn't alter the fact that he'd had to ring Zoe and break the news to her that this time the job had gone to someone else. She'd been OK about it really.

'It's all right,' she said, sounding only slightly disappointed. 'My time will come.'

Rory got up from the table, left the pub and went home to Sussex to potter in his greenhouse. It was nearly empty, because of the time of year, but somehow he knew that his cacti collection and over-wintering plants might not be enough to delete Annabel Grainger from his memory.

2

It was typical March weather and after the first day's shooting Annabel felt cold, grubby and completely exhausted. At the end of the day, when they all collected together in the nearest pub in order to unwind a little, she found herself hardly able to stand up straight.

Emma looked at her with sympathy in her eyes.

'You look a bit fed up, very fed up,' she amended as Annabel leaned heavily against the bar and yawned.

Although smiling was the last thing she felt like doing, Annabel suddenly caught sight of Rory's reflection in the mirror over the bar. He was watching her with a barely-concealed expression of triumph on his face so she forced her frozen lips to stretch from a yawn into the semblance of a grin.

'Oh, I'm OK,' she said. 'Just a bit cold.'

'Don't know what got into him,' Emma went on, shrugging in the direction of Rory. 'I mean, we all know he likes to get it right, but to make you do a retake in these temperatures was unreasonable. Little short of torture, if you ask me.'

'Oh, I don't know.' Annabel was determined to sound reasonable. 'Apparently, I filled the pots too full and didn't firm them down enough. A matter of opinion, really, but I'll soon get used to his ways.'

There was a movement behind her.

'Actually, it's not a matter of opinion, it's more a matter of continuity.'

Slowly, she turned round. Rory had appeared behind her. His shirt collar was open under his jacket and showed his strong neck. Annabel found herself staring fascinated at a place just above his collarbone where a pulse was working. She looked up, met his eyes and felt the heat flood into her face.

'I expect you're right,' she muttered,

struggling to regain her cool.

'No expect about it. I am right. You've no idea the number of letters we receive, telling us how three weeks ago we recommended filling the pots to about a quarter inch from the top, and yet last week we filled them to the brim.'

Annabel closed her eyes. Was there no pleasing this man? Did he have to make an issue out of everything, where she was concerned? For some reason she wasn't quite sure of, he wanted to give her a hard time, a really hard time.

She opened her eyes again. He was not going to win. She knew she'd put in a hard, professional day's work and that most people on the shoot agreed with her. Colin, the cameraman, had told her, well done; Andy, the trainee, had blushed every time she'd gone near him and helped her in every way he knew how. Emma, who was young and sweet besides being desperately in love with the cameraman, had soon struck up a friendly working relationship with her.

It seemed Rory was the only one she hadn't pleased.

Emma, she realised, had made her way across to the other side of the bar in order to join Colin. She watched as Colin draped an unselfconscious arm over her shoulders and started nuzzling her ear gently. For some reason, watching such cosiness made her feel very lonely. Impatiently, she wrenched her attention back to the man facing her. After all, she was a newcomer and this was her first day. She was bound to feel like an outsider at first. She lifted her chin and looked squarely into Rory's eyes. They looked cold and steely.

'Well, how did I do?' she asked tentatively.

It was Rory's turn to look surprised. After a moment, he rasped the back of his strong, tanned fingers against his square jaw as though feeling whether or not he needed a shave.

'You don't need me to tell you that.'

'Oh, but I do,' Annabel answered. 'I

mean, I know it's early days, but if you feel you've made a mistake in hiring me, I'd rather know straight away, not prolong the agony.'

'Well, let's see now.' He pretended to consider. 'You were here on time, followed directions to the letter, moved well with the camera, developed an instant rapport with the whole crew, didn't whinge once in spite of the cold, ignored the rumbling of Andy's stomach on more than one occasion . . . '

Annabel grinned. She thought she'd been the only one to notice that.

'Yes,' Rory went on, the seriousness of his voice belying the spark of humour in his eyes. 'I'd say you did OK, for the first day, that is.'

Stupidly, Annabel looked away, blinking back tears of tiredness and relief as she did so. She had so much wanted this job and so much wanted Rory's approval, although, why, she couldn't have said. After all, he'd spent the whole day bossing her about, making her do take after take, with never a word of encouragement or so much as a smile in her direction.

'And,' he continued, 'on top of that lot, you had to put up with me and my patronising, uncouth ways. Must have been a struggle for someone so out of the top drawer.'

Annabel stiffened. Why couldn't he have left it there? Why did he have to spoil it?

'Why do you do that?' she asked before she could stop herself.

Rory's steely eyes continued to bore straight through her.

'Do what?' he asked as he took a swig from his pint.

'Keep on about my coming out of the top drawer, as you like to put it.'

He shot her a penetrating glance.

'Well, it's true, isn't it? Everything's been easy for you so far. Right father and mother, right school, right university, right friends, right looks, right figure.' He stopped to give her an appraising inspection from head to toe. 'All adds up to the right job, right?'

The tide of fury which swept through Annabel threatened to knock her off her feet.

'Wrong,' she said, barely able to get the words out from her shaking lips. 'Very wrong on one.'

Rory raised a cynical eyebrow.

'Oh, yes, and which one's that?'

'I had the right mother all right, only she died when I was four, so I didn't have her for long. When she died, things weren't right for a long time, I can tell you.'

For a moment, Rory's expression was so stricken, Annabel almost felt a stirring of sympathy, but the fury was still there and the frustrations of keeping herself calm throughout the long, taxing day were too much.

'What right have you to judge me? You know nothing about me. I've just put in a gruelling day's work, so judge me on that if you're so keen on judging people. Leave my personal life out of it. As far as I'm concerned, you're running the show and I'll do my best to be professional, but that's it. I want this job and I'm prepared to give it my best shot, but from now on, I don't want any more to do with you than I have to.'

Annabel slammed down her glass on the bar and pushed her way out through the warm, noisy pub to the cold carpark outside.

Rory turned up the collar of his jacket. Stupid woman! How on earth was he to know her mother died when she was so young? He bit his lip. He knew he shouldn't have said what he'd said, shouldn't have gone on about the way she'd wangled her way on to the programme — his programme.

Women! They were a pain. Sighing, he put his empty glass back on the bar, then blinked in surprise because there, on the bar top, next to Annabel's glass was a small black leather pouch containing car keys. Rory picked them up. She wouldn't get far without these.

He gave a half smile. Now, should he make her eat humble pie and come back into the pub for them? His smile faded. No, not even he could do that. She'd looked so furious and amazingly beautiful with her face flushed, her lips trembling and her eyes flashing. No, he'd have to go find her. He hunched his shoulders and, pocketing the keys, strode through the pub after her.

She was fumbling in her bag when he found her. The light was poor and the bag was deep. Rory was half tempted to let her carry on her fruitless search, but no, that really wouldn't be fair. Before he could change his mind, he tapped her on the shoulder. She turned a tear-stained face towards him and his heart turned over. Gently he traced one of the tears down the line of her cheek with his finger. Her skin was so smooth. He'd made her cry. What a brute he was.

'I'm sorry,' he said, even though it was not something he said very often. 'I really am. I was a pig.'

Annabel shrank away from his touch as though scalded, then stuck out her chin defiantly.

'Yes, you were, and now I can't find

my keys either, so that just finishes off a perfect day really.'

They were standing just inches apart. Rory could see Annabel catching her lower lip between her teeth before she bent her head again to resume her search.

'Here are your keys, Annabel,' he said.

She looked up and the tremulous smile she gave him made his breath snag in his throat.

'Thanks. I suppose I left them in the pub. Not the sort of thing I usually do.'

She leaned towards him to retrieve them. Her hair brushed his cheek and fingers, searching for the keys, found his and suddenly he'd lost his mind because he was kissing her. Her mouth was warm and moist beneath his and a fire had started somewhere in the pit of his stomach.

Business and pleasure don't mix, his thoughts raced. This is a professional relationship, keep it that way. She's not interested in you. Daddy must already have his sights on the right man for his darling daughter. Rory Oakhurst is definitely not the right man. All these thoughts chased round in his mind before the passion of the kiss made further reasoning impossible.

It was hard to say who had pulled away first, Rory thought to himself afterwards, but it was definitely Annabel who kept her cool.

'OK,' she said panting a little bit, other than that appearing hardly ruffled. 'Now we've done that once, we don't have to do it again, do we? I'm tired. I'm going home for a nice shower and I'll see you in the morning.'

Not quite sure whether or not he was dreaming, Rory was left in the carpark imagining Annabel's beautiful face, not to mention delectable body, with rivulets of water running down it as she took her shower.

Annabel was not actually quite so calm as Rory imagined. Although she'd managed to sweep out of the carpark as though she were as cool as a cucumber, now she was on the road she found herself sitting bolt upright, gripping the steering wheel as though her life depended on it.

Calm, Annabel, calm, she told herself. But her lips were bruised and her body was burning as though she was in for a bout of flu. That was it, she wasn't well. She was tired and thoroughly chilled from the day's work, and then the drink in the heated atmosphere of the pub, standing at the bar instead of sitting, allowing Rory to upset her, when all the time she knew she shouldn't let him have the ability to affect her in any way whatsoever had done her no good. Rushing out into the cold carpark had added to it, and to cap it all, losing her keys. It had all added up to enough stress to make her reactions go into overdrive making her feel — well, not quite herself. What she needed was a nice, hot shower, the familiarity of her own flat and a square meal inside her. She'd feel normal enough again then.

As for the kiss! Annabel's face heated up again at the thought. That was all it was, just a kiss. Rory probably kissed loads of women. It was maybe his way of saying sorry.

After the kiss, what had she said? Annabel half closed her eyes and squirmed as she remembered — well, now we've done that once, we don't have to do it again! It made it sound like she'd taken it seriously or something, when anyone with any sense would know straight away that Rory was hardly the kind of guy to take one kiss seriously.

But Annabel couldn't help remembering that kiss because it had been unlike any other kiss she'd experienced. How could a kiss from such cold lips be warm and sweet and magical? How could a kiss from someone who'd just said such terrible things to her make her melt and yield and respond in a way she'd never believed was possible?

Her face was burning again and her hands trembling so much at the memory that she had to grip the steering wheel harder than ever and force herself to put Rory Oakhurst out of her mind. For the rest of the drive home, Annabel concentrated hard on her driving and when she finally arrived, after a shower and hastily-prepared cheese sandwich, she fell into bed exhausted.

Three hours later, she was awake again. She stirred slowly, stretching herself like a cat. She'd been dreaming of something wonderful. A smile lifted the corners of her mouth. The dream was coming tantalisingly close. What was it? She'd been in a cornfield, running through golden ears of corn and blood red poppies at thigh height. She was laughing and happy because there was someone behind her, someone whom she cared about, a lot.

She could feel the heat of his body as he caught her close from behind, felt a deep stirring within her as with one hand on her waist, the other on her breast, he turned her to face him. Still smiling, she lifted her face for his kiss. Her eyes were closed as he gently lowered her to the ground. Hungrily, she opened her mouth beneath his. She was drowning in his kiss.

Annabel opened her eyes, and sat bolt upright in bed.

'No,' she gasped. 'No, no, no!'

★ ★ ★

As the day's shoot had been in the Sussex show garden, Rory didn't have such a long drive home. He had a pub meal with the others and afterwards stayed there longer than usual, putting off the time when he would finally be in just his own company and unable to avoid thinking about Annabel Grainger.

'What happened to Annabel then?' Emma asked.

Along with Colin, she was one of the last to leave. Rory looked away from Emma's open gaze.

'I thought I told you once. She

suddenly remembered something she had to do.'

'Yeah, that's right, and she forgot her car keys and you went running after her, I remember.'

'Right.'

'If you say so.'

It was obvious she didn't believe him. Rory sighed and turned back to his pint.

'Annabel's nice,' Emma said quietly, 'really nice. Not a bit toffee nosed and she mucks in and fetches the tea the same as anyone else. I bet you upset her. You're being too hard on her. She's probably scared enough of you anyway. I know I was when I started. She winked at Colin as she added, 'I didn't know then that you were really a pussy cat.'

Rory wanted to smile, but instead set his mouth in a thin hard line.

'Pussy cat or not, I'll do any worrying that's to be done about Annabel and I want you on set on time tomorrow or you're fired! OK?'

Tucking her arm in Colin's, Emma gave a last grin as she went out of the door.

Rory didn't stay long after that. There was no point, he told himself, because now that Emma had made him think about Annabel Grainger he found nothing could make him stop. He recalled the way she'd worked so hard today, the way she'd fitted in easily with the other crew members, the fact that despite his being unreasonably awkward to please, she'd just gritted her teeth and got on with it; the way, in fact, that although he'd been trying to make her regret taking the job, she'd stuck it out and passed every test with flying colours.

But Emma was wrong. Annabel wasn't scared of him. Remembering the way her eyes had blazed fire at him when she'd told him she'd do her job but wanted as little possible to do with him on a personal level, he gave a rueful grin. Oh, no, she certainly wasn't scared of him.

His grin faded. He, on the other hand, if he was truthful about it, was more than a little scared of her, or rather, scared of the effect she had on him, of her softness and her sudden vulnerability. He was scared senseless by the way that kiss had made him feel. Rory half closed his eyes for a moment as he recalled the deep stirring of passion the kiss had brought to the surface.

Fifteen minutes later, it was with a start that he realised he had reached the cottage. Fifteen minutes of fantasising. What was wrong with him? A kiss was just a kiss. People did it all the time. Just forget it Rory, like you have so many others. He swung his feet out of the car and on to the gravel and crunched his way to the heavy oak front door.

It was good to be back in his own space. Soon he was in his farmhouse-style kitchen, avoiding the bunches of drying hops that hung from the low-slung rafters. He filled the kettle, and took a mug from the cupboard. A nice cup of strong tea, that was what he needed. Perhaps Emma was right. Rather than trying to prove that Annabel was getting no special treatment, from him at any rate, maybe he should just back off now, pretend she was no different from anyone else, because, after all, she wasn't, was she? In spite of that kiss!

3

The next day, Annabel could hardly believe the normality of Rory's behaviour to everyone and her in particular. She had expected there to be at least a coolness between them, but after no more than a good-morning nod to everyone, Rory took charge and they continued where they'd left off the day before.

The weather was better but threatened to break, so there was even less time for mistakes, but they did well and pretty soon everything had been covered, even to Rory's satisfaction. They wound up early and this time only a few of them went to the pub.

'I'd like a word, Annabel,' Rory said after the pub meal and just as she was struggling into her coat.

Annabel felt her heart lurch. What had she done now?

'What's the problem?' she asked when they were sitting facing one another on either side of a roaring fire in a quieter corner of the pub.

'No problem. I just wanted to congratulate you on two very good days filming. I know it's not all new to you, but it's still difficult to fit in with an already functioning team and grapple with the elements. You've done well.'

Try as she might, Annabel couldn't quell the warm tide of happiness welling up inside her. But praise from Rory was so rare. She looked at him suspiciously.

'Spare my blushes, please,' she said to cover her confusion. 'You've got a good team. They made it easy for me.'

'Well, I didn't,' he admitted. 'I was too hard on you yesterday, Annabel, and I apologise. I'm sure you are the right person for the job and if I gave you any reason to think otherwise by my behaviour yesterday then again, I apologise. I'm sure you'll agree, things have gone very well today so I hope we can consider it a fresh start.'

His eyes met hers for a moment and she read a certain wariness in his expression. He's as nervous as I am, she realised. Either that or he's scared that if he's offended me enough to make me quit, he'll be in big trouble with Sebastian. A mischievous gleam came into her eyes.

'I knew the first couple of days might be . . . ' She paused, choosing her words carefully. 'Well, unpredictable, but I'm sure things will work out. After all, we're both professional people. We both know you can't get on with all of the people all of the time, but I can certainly get on with most of the people most of the time — and I don't find it an effort.'

She smiled. She could see that Rory was trying in vain to read her expression. Her smile broadened. It really was fun to keep him guessing.

He rasped his hand across his chin again. She noticed he did that when he wasn't sure what to say.

43

'I'll get you another drink,' he offered eventually. 'White wine, wasn't it?'

'Dry, please.'

'Right.'

Two drinks later, the second only soda water because of the driving, they were still sitting opposite one another, still talking, still eyeing one another a trifle warily, but at least, Annabel kept reminding herself, they were communicating.

At Rory's invitation, she'd been describing her father's Gloucestershire garden. She outlined the way they'd designed a laburnum-covered walkway, explained the problems they'd had with drainage and the sunken garden idea that just hadn't worked out.

'Now, how about you?'

She smiled across at him watching the way he drummed his fingers on the table top whenever there was a lull in the conversation and noticing the strength in his tanned fingers as he did so.

'Me? Oh, you mean my garden. Well,

it's small by your sort of standards, I expect. Untamed and unkempt, I'm ashamed to admit. But there are wild rhodies on two sides, in the spring drifts of daffodils, the small native ones, and down at the bottom there's a bank of primroses and, of course, the stream.'

'A stream? You mean to tell me there's a real stream?' Annabel couldn't hide her delight. 'You lucky devil. Dad's got a sort of pond. Well, I suppose it's more than a pond, really.'

'You mean a lake,' Rory interrupted.

'No, I don't. I mean a large pond, well, all right, very large, with a sort of bridge thing where it narrows. But it's nothing like as exciting as a natural stream. Do you sit on the edge and dangle your feet in?'

'Not lately, no. Hardly the weather.'

Annabel pulled a face.

'Yes, I'd noticed. I didn't think filming in March would be as cold as this. Is it usually this bad or is it because I'm not used to being outside in it for quite so long at a stretch?'

Rory grinned.

'Bit of both, I'm afraid. But let's not talk about the weather.'

Annabel leaned forward in anticipation. He was going to discuss them, how fabulously well they were getting on. He was remembering that kiss and going to ask her out for dinner or something.

'About these assignments for the programme,' he said.

Her smile died immediately. She should have guessed. It was back to business. He'd been softening her up. Goodness knows what he'd got lined up for her.

'For some time,' Rory started, 'we've been trying to pull off an interview with Lawrence Beardsley at Beardsley Grange, his home near the New Forest.'

'Ye-es,' Annabel prompted tentatively.

Lawrence Beardsley was a minor aristocrat whose name appeared regularly in the gossip columns, and who was making a name for himself as a style guru with an eye to becoming a garden designer, the kind Annabel wouldn't have thought Rory would have much time for.

'Well, up until now he's not been very encouraging. I'm maybe too down to earth for him. I've never met the man but for some reason what he's seen of me on the box doesn't seem to have endeared me to him.'

'I wonder why that could be,' Annabel asked innocently, all the while thinking to herself it was probably that next to Rory, Lawrence Beardsley would undoubtedly look the wimp that he was, and wouldn't take too kindly to the comparison showing on screen for all to see.

'It seems that Sebastian and he move in the same circles, and once it was mentioned that you might be going to do some interviews for us. Well, let's say he's now changed his tune and seems quite keen.'

Thinking that if this were the case, then Sebastian must have made the decision to take her on even before the interview. Annabel was unsure how to react, so she did what she knew she was good at. She smiled.

'Well, what do you think?' he asked.

'I think things are moving pretty fast, as regards the programme, I mean,' she added hurriedly.

'I take it you know him, socially, I mean.'

'We were once at the same wedding,' Annabel said, her smile slightly frozen now at the memory.

'Great. That gives you the perfect way in.'

Not quite perfect, Annabel thought. No, not quite.

'You see,' Rory said, the belligerent gleam back in his eyes. 'I'm right, aren't I?'

'How's that?'

'Well, here you are, two days in the job and you've practically landed our first really big interview. I mean Beardsley Grange Gardens are just amazing, and none of the other programmes have had him yet. You'll get extra Brownie points with Sebastian for this. Come on, even you have to admit it's all a question of whom you know.'

Annabel could feel a needle of irritation beginning to aggravate her.

'If that's the case, how on earth did you get anywhere? If you'll forgive my saying so, you're a bit short in the charm department and you didn't have any of my so-called advantages. So how did you manage to end up with your own successful gardening show? Impossible, you said.'

A frown came over Rory's features and his eyes turned to chips of ice.

'I worked damn hard, that's how.'

'Oh, and luck had nothing to do with it, then? You're the only one who's got anywhere by hard work alone, are you?'

He shrugged. Annabel laughed.

'My goodness! You're a snob, that's what you are.'

Rory's hand shot out across the table and held her wrist in an iron-like grip.

'That's one thing I'm not. Don't you

ever, ever call me a snob. How dare you?'

Fiercely, Annabel stared back at him.

'Oh, I dare, all right, because a snob is exactly what you are. You seem to think anyone who hasn't had to struggle too much can't possibly have a shred of talent. You're a snob all right, and what's more, you're an inverted snob and that's the worst kind!'

Now I've done it, she thought. He really hates me now!

Fuming, Rory drove too fast all the way home. A snob, an inverted snob? How dare she call him that! How dare she! Slowly Rory had let out an expulsion of breath.

'OK, so that's what you think. Fine.'

After that, they'd sat there in a silence that Rory was determined he would not be the first to break.

'Sorry,' Annabel said finally. 'I don't know what it is about us. We just don't deal together well, do we?'

Then she'd smiled that really terrific smile of hers and all his anger had melted and his heart had started beating big time. And then what had he said?

'You're right. Were right — the first time. Let's keep this strictly business, keep our personal thoughts to ourselves. This Beardsley Grange Gardens project is such an opportunity for all of us, we can't afford for it to go wrong just because we're at each other's throats and don't even know why.'

Only he did know why. No amount of pompous speechmaking was going to alter the fact that he, Rory Oakhurst, whose rule had always been love them and leave them, was finding that with Annabel, in spite of their chaste, professional relationship, he was finding it difficult to keep things cool. For a start, that smile. It started harmlessly enough, but by the time Rory realised just what it was doing to him, it was too late to put his defences in place. So then what happened? He over-reacted, pretended he couldn't stand her smile, that her way of saying exactly what she thought really gave him the ache and the next thing he knew, they'd be arguing.

Just like tonight, in fact, when they'd finished their drinks in silence and, hardly looking at one another, politely said good-night. And now, here he was, driving too fast, just because he'd give anything to go back to that pub, hold her hand gently, instead of nearly breaking her arm, and say, 'Annabel, you're the most beautiful girl I've ever seen in my life and I think I'm falling in love with you.'

Rory groaned out loud. Get a grip. Taking life too seriously didn't get anybody anywhere. What he needed was a good night out, a nice, uncomplicated happy time knocking back a few drinks, having a bit of a laugh — just an old-fashioned good time. He'd have to arrange it, fast, before Annabel wormed her way any further into his affections.

His driving slowed down and a grin spread itself across his face. Zoe

Blackstop! It was a few weeks since he'd seen her. He had a couple of jobs he could put her way, and he knew he owed her. Zoe was so straightforward, not the kind of girl to set your pulses racing, more of a mate really. Come to think of it, he could send her with Annabel to Beardsley Grange as her assistant. He'd been going to go himself only to lurk in the background and give Annabel back-up where she needed it.

He was astute enough to know that he and Lawrence Beardsley would never really make a good combination. Lawrence had the reputation as a bit of a ladies' man. He'd probably be chuffed to bits to have not one but two attractive women sent to dance attendance on him. Annabel and Zoe would make a good team. It would be a one off, good for both of them. They might strike up a friendship. After all, they had a lot in common. They both liked gardening and they were both female!

Yes, the interview would be a success. Annabel with her charm and her contacts and Zoe with her expertise on the gardening side. He could virtually bow out, give himself a break, do a bit of forward planning on other projects in the pipeline, take his mind right off Annabel for a while.

Pleased with himself, Rory smirked a little. All it took was a little calm, reflective thought and a little discipline. He could put Annabel to the back of his mind, no trouble.

4

It was the first week in May. Annabel had never known time to go so quickly. By now, the team had taken her to their hearts and she no longer felt herself to be an outsider. Throughout April, the **Dig Your Garden** ratings had crept upwards slowly, but Rory said that happened at this time of year anyway, so Annabel knew it could have nothing to do with her.

However, she had to admit to herself that it was gratifying when colleagues stopped her and said how much they enjoyed the show, or a particular piece she'd been involved in. Rory, as ever, was bent on the next project in the show's garden and spent little time gloating over past glories. He preferred to concentrate on the work of the future.

And now the time had come for the

Lawrence Beardsley interview. Even though she knew she owed a lot of her luck to the fact that by chance, Lawrence appeared to prefer her style of interviewing to that of Rory, she was delighted by the fact that it was her big opportunity to go it alone.

'Good luck,' Rory said to her the day before she left for the New Forest with her team. 'Take as much footage as you like, but remember, the garden is the star of the show. I know Lawrence Beardsley is never out of the gossip columns but we're a gardening show.'

Annabel opened her mouth to say she was well aware of that, but found herself thanking him instead for the chance he was giving her.

'We'll do a good job,' she said. 'We won't let you down, I promise.'

Over the last few weeks, all the preparation prior to the event had been completed. The camera crew knew what the set-up was. In the introduction, Annabel and Lawrence were to stroll casually amongst the rhododendrons and azaleas, stopping here and there as though by accident, in order to discuss a particularly fine and interesting specimen.

Together, Annabel and Zoe had explored the area they were going to cover, picked out the most obvious specimens for discussion, looked them up in the books, checked and double checked that names and pronunciation were correct. Then Zoe had checked again for any problems, pets or conditions that would affect the plant's performance. It was all fairly standard procedure, but one that Annabel had not been solely responsible for previously.

'Hi,' Zoe said warmly when they had first met five weeks ago. 'You beat me to it.'

Annabel looked puzzled. Zoe grinned and shrugged.

'The job. Your job, I should say. Thought I had it in the bag till you showed up. Still,' she said and held out her hand, 'no hard feelings. I'm probably better suited to freelancing anyway.'

Annabel shook the small but strong hand held out to her. So this was the girl that Rory had favoured for the presenting job. Well, she seemed pleasant enough in a boyish way, and with her straight, shining red hair and cheerful grin, she was certainly attractive.

They'd worked together a couple of times since then, but their main joint task had been the setting up of the Beardsley Grange project. However, although Annabel couldn't put her finger on it, and Zoe seemed friendly enough, there was something about Zoe's manner she couldn't quite take to. But they worked together well and certainly there was less tension between them than there was between Annabel and Rory, although even that seemed to have lessened of late, Annabel realised.

Today was the day the cameras would roll. There was a fluttering in Annabel's stomach. She knew just how important it was to succeed on this, her first big undertaking. It had absolutely nothing to do with impressing Rory Oakhurst, she told herself, absolutely nothing at all.

The journey to the edge of the New Forest had been very pleasant. It was a wonderful time of year what with the scent of bluebells, abundant wild rhododendrons just bursting into flower, and lush green foliage. They'd booked into their modest accommodation then made themselves familiar with the gardens of Beardsley Grange. The walk-throughs and rehearsals had to take place in Lawrence's absence, however. He'd been tied up with more important obligations.

'That's pretty typical,' Annabel couldn't resist saying.

Zoe glanced at her beneath sooty lashes which owed their darkness to lavish helpings of mascara, the only make-up she aspired to.

'It sounds as though you don't care too much for Lawrence.'

Briefly, Annabel tossed up whether to keep mum about her previous experience of Lawrence's charms. Zoe had an earthy sexiness about her that Lawrence might take as a come-on.

'He's very sure of himself,' she said at last because she felt that even though Zoe gave every appearance of being able to look after herself, Lawrence would have no qualms about forcing himself where he wasn't wanted. 'I expect you've heard his reputation. I think it's probably all too terribly true.'

'Really?' Zoe's eyes widened. 'I've never been introduced to him. Too big a hot shot for the likes of me, but I've always thought he looked quite tasty.'

Annabel gulped in amazement. Lawrence Beardsley, tasty? She supposed that in a reptilian way he may be considered good-looking, but surely as soon as you spoke to the guy, you knew he was just a spoiled bully, out to impress by setting the newest fashion tends and sporting the latest 'it' girl on his arm.

'I should reserve judgement till you meet him,' she said.

As if on cue, the owner of Beardsley Grange ambled into the conservatory where Annabel's conversation with Zoe was taking place.

Lawrence was not much above average height and skinny enough to pass for elegant on the TV screen. This morning he was looking decidedly the worse for wear. Although it was barely ten o'clock, he was carrying a flute of what looked like champagne and was wearing the latest designer sunglasses. His hair was in fashionable disarray, but all the backcombing in the world couldn't disguise the fact that he was thinning on top.

Not his fault, Annabel thought. Nevertheless, remembering how it had felt to be cornered by him, she struggled to suppress a shudder of distaste. Lawrence, however, seemed to recall none of Annabel's unpleasant memories.

'Annabel, darling,' he drawled. 'Just

so fabulous to see you, yah?'

Dutifully, Annabel held out a hand and smiled. Lawrence ignored the hand and homed in for a continental double kiss greeting. With only the smallest of winces, Annabel complied.

'Like you to met Zoe Blackstop, assistant on the shoot,' she said hurriedly when she was released.

True to form, Lawrence closed in for another clinch. Zoe was pressed up against Lawrence's none-too-clean shirtfront. Annabel wondered vaguely, if there was any way she could get him to change it for the cameras, without him thinking she was after his body.

'Terrif,' Lawrence said, eyeing Zoe up and down. 'Anyone for bubbly?'

Three hours later, Annabel sat in the conservatory once again, only this time she was alone. She pressed her hand to her temples. The last three hours had been like trial by fire.

Lawrence had been a pain. He'd objected to most of the shots they'd set up, insisted that the main part of the interview be conducted by the herb-aceous border, because it was the most famous part of the garden, never mind that at this time of year everything was in bud and needed another couple of weeks before it would be ready. Also he'd interrupted and corrected Annabel at every opportunity.

'I think you'll find my way's best, darling. Terrif.'

Exasperated almost beyond endur-ance, Annabel eventually told the film crew to keep the camera rolling at all times in the hope that somehow she'd have enough decent footage amongst the dross to salvage a reasonable interview.

'I didn't realise he was to be in charge,' Zoe said with a sly grin.

Annabel gave a rueful smile.

'He isn't, but he has to think he is. Believe me, he can be even nastier if he's crossed.'

Zoe raised her brows and Annabel had neither the time nor the inclination to puzzle out the meaning behind the gesture.

Now, due to a sudden but brief shower of rain, they were having a short lunchbreak and Annabel was studying her notes and the questions she'd prepared for the final, more formal interview to be conducted in the fernery. Lawrence had been adamant that his pet project was to feature largely in the interview.

'The fernery is just so magnificent right now. The fabulous new growth's coming through and the greens are just to die for.'

On viewing the oasis of calm and inspiration, with its gently-flowing stream trickling over rocks covered with mosses, unusual ferns and lichens, Annabel had to agree. The fernery did look wonderful and if they could catch the sunlight filtering through the trees on to the magnificent blue-green ferns, it would make a stunning closing sequence. So the location had been chosen. She just had to go over her notes once more.

'Ah, it's the beautiful Annabel.'

Oh, no! Annabel tried to change her

stricken expression to one of welcome, for Lawrence, complete with two full champagne glasses, stood on the threshold of the conservatory.

'Now I know you said all that boring stuff about not drinking on the job, but come on. It's lunchtime. A drop of champers isn't going to hurt, darling.'

'I'd rather not, honestly.'

'Sit down and relax, darling. You look a little tense, yah?'

Before she knew it, Lawrence had slithered his way round to the back of her and she felt his fingers massaging her neck and shoulders. A shiver of revulsion passed through her.

'It's OK, really,' she stammered. 'I really think we should go down to the fernery and have a preliminary run-through.'

Lawrence ignored her and continued to dig his fingers into her top vertebrae.

'You know, I've thought about you so often since the last time,' he murmured into her ear.

Last time? What last time? She supposed he must be referring to the quick grope he'd had when he cornered her in a secluded alcove at the wedding of the year. Remembering it now, and how she'd elbowed him sharply in the chest before running for it, she gritted her teeth and closed her eyes to rid herself of the nausea the memory evoked.

'Uh-oh . . . sorry.'

Annabel opened her eyes to see Zoe, complete with clipboard, staring at them with unabashed curiosity.

'Sorry,' she said again. 'I thought you were on your own, Annabel.'

Relief washed through Annabel, but it didn't stop her face from flushing.

'We're just going down to the fernery for a quick rehearsal.'

A snigger came from Lawrence.

'Well, I've heard it called other things.' He put his hands up mockingly. 'But I surrender, darling. You know I'm a push-over for you — anything you say — yah?'

'Very funny, Lawrence,' Annabel replied in a voice which she hoped was jokey, not disdainful. 'But I'd really like to catch the light before it goes.'

'That's what I came to tell you,' Zoe said. 'Colin's set up down there, says the light's perfect right now. I believe he's taking more back-up shots in case it breaks.'

Zoe was right. When they reached the fernery, the whole of the glade was bathed in a magical, slightly-eerie light. The crew was already there, ready to roll.

'Give us a minute's run-through time,' Annabel said and turned to Lawrence. 'Now I'm going to ask you for a brief history of the fernery, how you came to think of setting it out, the problems you encountered, that sort of thing. Then we'll go on to talk about some of the ferns and the different conditions they need. I know my boss, Rory, will be interested to see this part of the interview. Ferns are a bit of a specialty of his.'

Lawrence's face stiffened.

'I hardly think so,' he drawled. 'That jumped-up amateur, he couldn't tell the difference between a fern and a piece of bracken.'

Annabel couldn't believe she was hearing correctly.

'Pardon?' she said coldly. 'I think you must be confusing him with somebody else. It's well-known that Rory is an authority in the field of ferns, lichens and mosses, grasses, too, for that matter. In fact, he's extremely knowledgeable in any area of plant life you care to mention.'

For a moment, Lawrence looked nonplussed, then his face broke into a wolfish grin.

'My dear girl,' he said with the drawl in his voice that Annabel had come to hate, 'you clearly don't know what you're speaking about. Rory Oakhurst has been extremely lucky, that's all. He's had next to no education, is singularly lacking in any social graces and what's more, doesn't have a spark of talent. He's hardly an authority on anything.'

Zoe dropped her clipboard, and there was a long silence. Annabel could feel the crew members holding their breath. Hold on, Annabel, count to ten. OK then, maybe fifteen. Don't let him get to you, don't lost your temper or you'll louse up for everyone. She smiled sweetly.

'Well, we're all entitled to our own opinions, but to get back to your expertise, Lawrence, after all, that's what we're after. Perhaps you could point out a few of your favourites and explain what it is about them that you particularly like.'

Annabel heard a hiss as the crew members all let out their breath simultaneously. Lawrence preened himself a little, then started to expound on his extensive fern collection. Annabel relaxed. She'd kept control, been professional, even though what she'd have most liked to do was punch Lawrence Beardsley on the nose.

★ ★ ★

Rory put the final cassette in the video machine. He'd asked to see all the footage even though he'd seen the final version of the interview and was happy with it.

He already had a very clear idea what made Lawrence tick — power, money, affectation and bullying, but he wasn't interested in Lawrence's personality, only his garden, and his garden was truly magnificent. Surely, Rory reasoned to himself, the bloke had to have some redeeming qualities to have kept this little lot going, leave alone adding all the extra features, like the fernery, that worked so well.

The video flickered in front of him. The woodland walk was winding its way before him, camellias, rhododendrons and azaleas almost vulgar in their brilliance. Lawrence and Annabel were sauntering along stopping randomly it seemed, to comment on a striking combination of colour, or a particularly impressive bloom. Lawrence was rather closer to Annabel than necessary, Rory thought, and did he have to smile that wolfish grin quite so often? And really, the way he ended everything he said with 'yah' and a question mark, was enough to drive anybody mad.

But the garden, that was something else. For a moment, Rory was wildly jealous that Annabel had got to see all this, while he was only witnessing it second hand, but then as he watched, he recognised that Lawrence was the type to respond more generously to a woman. Yes, that was probably why he'd insisted on Annabel conducting the interview. It probably wasn't anything personal against him, Rory, in particular, he just preferred working with women, especially someone as beautiful as Annabel, and who could blame him for that?

Momentarily, Rory's breath was taken away. Colin's shot of that clear golden light that occurs only immediately after rain when the skies opposite are still leaden, filled the screen. Slowly the camera panned through the trees, picking out shafts of light as they bathed the cool blue-green fronds of the ferns. Wow! He was just about to replay the shot when it changed to include Annabel and Lawrence just prior to the final interview.

'I know my boss, Rory, will be interested to see this part of the interview. Ferns are a bit of a specialty of his,' Annabel was saying.

Lawrence's face stiffened.

'I hardly think so,' he drawled. 'That jumped-up amateur, he couldn't tell the difference between a fern and a piece of bracken.'

With an expressionless face, Rory watched the rest of the interview, then he rewound it and watched it again. He let out a roar of laughter. That Lawrence character — what a prize buffoon. His laugh subsided. He had to admit Annabel had handled the whole thing brilliantly.

His rather harsh profile softened as

he played back the scene for a third time. Yes, she really had looked very angry there for a moment, very angry indeed, but she'd managed to control it, return the interview on to an even footing. She's amazing, he thought, and perhaps she does like me just a little bit after all.

5

The run-up to the Chelsea Flower Show was one of the most frantic times Annabel had experienced. The media, already inundated with gardening information, seemed to have an unquenchable thirst for even more. All this at a time when there was so much work to be done in the show garden.

'Awful weather isn't helping,' Rory growled.

It was true. After a not-too-bad April and early May, the weather had nose-dived, with warnings of heavy showers, high winds and light frosts. The **Dig Your Garden** team laboured on, filming inside when they could and outside when they couldn't avoid it with what felt like heavy downpours showing only as fine drizzle on the screen.

After two weeks of other freelance

work, Zoe was back on the scene. She'd been brought in as a familiar face to be seen in the vegetable patch.

'Is Zoe all right about this?' Annabel asked, picking up pretty quickly that Zoe was fiercely ambitious.

Rory's eyebrows shot up.

'What d'you mean? All right about what?'

'Well, she might feel she's being used. You know, we have a gap here. Whom can we use to fill it? Oh, yes, how about good old Zoe?'

Rory contemplated her for a long moment during which Annabel noted once again the particularly attractive grey of his eyes.

'Rubbish,' he said dismissively. 'Zoe would never be so small-minded. Anyway I had a long chat with her about the position and she levelled with me completely, said that although naturally she'd been disappointed that she didn't get the job, it certainly wouldn't stop her from helping out in whatever way she could. As long as she gets exposure, we pay her and she gets her name on the credits, she's more than willing to work for us.

Briefly, Annabel wondered if that particular conversation had taken place before or after Beardsley Grange.

The screening of Beardsley Grange Gardens had been a great success. Both Sebastian and her father had complimented Annabel on the programme. Rory, however, had complimented the whole team but, to her disappointment, failed to single her out for any special praise. Against all odds, Annabel knew that somehow, she had managed to portray Lawrence as a slightly eccentric, but charming gardening enthusiast, passionate about plants and interested in the future of the gardening masses. And, thanks to Colin's superb skills, the gardens had never appeared more spectacular.

'Lawrence should be on his bended knees thanking us,' Rory said. 'He received a hefty fee for the interview and the takings at his gate this year are going to be up by twenty per cent, I bet.'

Annabel was surprised.

'I had the impression he was rolling in it anyway. I thought this career thing was just another boost to his ego. You know — just a few more fans to add to his image.'

Rory frowned, then shrugged.

'You'd be more in a position to know about that. I just heard a whisper that his lifestyle costs rather more than his income allows.'

'Well, if he swilled a little less champagne, and worked a bit harder, he could remedy that.'

'Hmm!'

The Chelsea Flower Show was, as usual, to be covered mainly by the BBC who, by tradition, always had the first crack. But Rory's following on a rival channel was such that **Dig Your Garden** would be represented, and Rory himself would be conducting some interviews. Although he didn't say much, Annabel knew he was looking forward to it and felt in a way that it made up for him missing out on

Beardsley Grange.

Therefore, when Rory asked if she'd help out a little more than usual in the show garden to relieve the pressure, she was only too ready to oblige.

It had been a frustrating day. The tree fern they were going to plant in the fernery they were creating after the interest shown in the Beardsley Grange fernery turned up very late. Luckily the light was still good, even though most of the day had been overcast and quite cold.

Together, after Andy had dug the hole off camera, Rory and Annabel planted the tree fern. It was to be the last shot of the day.

'Wonder what Lawrence would think of this?' she queried when the cameras had stopped and they stood back to look at the effect.

A crinkle of amusement appeared at the corners of Rory's mouth.

'Well, he has a couple actually. The one he picked out on the programme and gave some fancy and totally incorrect name to, was in fact this very same tree fern. It's a silver tree fern from New Zealand.'

Annabel opened her eyes wide.

'I thought he was an expert.'

Rory's grin spread and he rasped his fingers across his chin.

'Yes, so did I till I saw that.'

'I'm sorry, I should have checked. It was the one area I thought it was safe to leave to him, but that's no excuse. I should have checked. Did anyone spot it?'

By now Rory was laughing openly.

'A few e-mails, that's all.'

'Well, what's so funny then?'

'There are eleven thousand fern species, world wide that is.'

'And?'

'Twenty eight thousand silver tree ferns come to the UK from New Zealand every year. That's how common it is. Lawrence had it in his own garden and couldn't even recognise it. Some expert he is!'

Annabel felt her mouth begin to curve upwards.

'Is he a complete fraud, d'you think?' she asked when she'd finished laughing.

Rory shrugged himself back into the old jacket he'd taken off while they'd been planting.

'No, he has a rudimentary knowledge, I'm sure. The trouble is, if you're stuck, it's no good waffling on television, because there's always someone out there who will spot it and when you're proved wrong it does your credibility no good whatsoever. What he should have done was admitted that the name of it had slipped his mind, or just glossed over it by commenting on how handsome the specimen was.'

Annabel started to feel anxious.

'Will the mistake reflect on the programme, d'you think?'

Rory ignored her question.

'It was a good job it was you with him and not me.'

'Why d'you say that?'

'Well, you know what I'm like. I'd have corrected him and we'd either have argued and then had to replay the whole thing, with him glowering at me, or he would have had to admit I was right and I somehow don't think he'd have done that, do you?'

Again Annabel grinned. Perhaps she had her uses after all.

She was still smiling half an hour later when they were preparing to leave the show garden. Rory was loading his gear into his car.

'I'm off,' she said, glancing at her watch. 'Goodness, it's later than I thought. I'm going to catch the traffic.'

Rory's dishevelled head emerged from the boot of his car.

'Tell you what,' he started, then he scratched his head and seemed to change his mind. 'No, not a good idea.'

No matter how hard she tried, Annabel found it impossible to read his expression. His face looked slightly pink, and his eyes rather bright. If it had been anyone else she would have said it was shyness, but shy was not a word she associated readily with Rory Oakhurst.

'Well, at least tell me, so I know what it is that isn't a good idea.'

Rory straightened up.

'It's just that once you expressed an interest in the stream at the bottom of my garden, and, well . . . ' He stopped and pushed the hair out of his eyes. 'Well, it does look particularly good right now. The primroses have more or less finished, of course, but there are forget-me-nots, bugle and mosses, the beginnings of the brooklime and purple loose strife and, of course, the wild irises.'

He broke off, looking awkward.

'Well, they're not really in flower yet, but it's such a wonderful time of year, so fresh, and at this time in the evening with the blackbirds singing enough to bust a gut and the sound of the stream — well, I like it, anyway.'

'Well, you've sold me,' Annabel said. 'I'd love to see it.'

Careful, she thought to herself. Don't sound too eager. You know what he's like. Just because he wants you to see his stream doesn't mean he wants the relationship to go any further. It's probably more a case of work experience. But Rory was smiling.

'Follow me then,' he said.

Nervously, Annabel climbed into her car. Maybe this wasn't such a good idea after all. She followed him out of the carpark and then very quickly lost sight of him as he roared away on what was obviously a familiar run for him. At the first traffic lights, she caught up with him again and tried to signal him to slow down because she was unsure which direction they were heading in. She wondered if he realised that if she lost sight of him she would be completely lost.

About twenty minutes later, they arrived at a small cottage.

'Here we are,' Rory greeted her as she opened her car door and swung her feet on to a driveway that was more mud than gravel.

'Come in,' he welcomed, opening the

oak door and half pushing her into the dimness ahead.

Annabel halted on the threshold.

'Well, this is . . . '

She paused, trying to accustom her eyes to the gloom.

'Charming,' she said eventually.

'I live pretty simply,' Rory explained glancing round the sparsely-furnished living area with pride. 'The kitchen's through here, but we'll go straight through to the garden, shall we?'

The kitchen turned out to be a little more welcoming than the sitting-room. It, too, had flagstones on the floor, a butler sink and several battered wooden cupboards and, slung from the beams, garlands of dried hops.

'This is very nice,' Annabel said with a little more spontaneity. 'I love dried hops.'

'Do you? My, er, sister informs me they're old hat, but I like them.'

His sister, Annabel thought. I bet that was a girlfriend!

By now, Rory was opening the back

door, which seemed to require a lift to almost bring it off its hinges before the key turned in the lock.

'Sorry,' he explained. 'The door's a little warped.'

'A bit like its owner, maybe,' Annabel quipped, smiling to show it was a joke.

But once he had the door open, Annabel gasped aloud at the view.

There was a very small courtyard paved with flagstones similar to those in the downstairs rooms and to one side was an old wooden bench and a small strip of earth filled with chives, parsley, thyme, sage and lavender. Behind that was a small greenhouse and directly in front of them, an arch covered in a climber that turned out to be where the hops had come from.

Beyond was an untamed stretch of grass with a rosy brick wall to the side covered with wisteria and a couple of early clematis. Crawling along the brokendown fence opposite was a laburnum mixed in a glorious muddle along with honeysuckle and climbing roses, neither of which were yet in flower. The garden faced west and as they stood there, a shaft of sun made its appearance at the edge of a sultry cloud.

'Wow,' Annabel said. 'I thought you said this was unkempt.'

Rory smiled a genuine smile of pleasure.

'It is unkempt, comparatively. It's what you might call low-maintenance. I've hardly any perennials, only the ones that can fend for themselves. I rely on a few herbs and climbers. I get poppies in the summer but that's about it really. I'd love to get some vegetables going, but I'd never have time to tend them properly, and it's hardly worth it for one.'

Annabel cast her eyes farther down the garden and walked purposefully through the hop-covered arch towards the end from where she could already hear the sound of water.

'Ah, the stream.'

Rory wasn't far behind her.

'You're so lucky, Rory.'

He grinned.

'I know. It's why I bought the place really.'

'I'm not surprised.'

Mesmerised, Annabel stood watching as the stream gurgled past, glinting and bubbling amongst the ferns, mosses and small boulders.

'Here, there's a seat.'

Rory took her arm and guided her to a bench, perched on the bank, that had certainly seen better days. Annabel sank down on to it and drank in the scene.

'I'll fetch a glass of wine, if you're not too cold out here. I'm afraid I've only got red.'

'Fine,' Annabel said not stirring.

It was so tranquil. Annabel watched as birds flew backwards and forwards across the stream.

'Here we are,' Rory said as he sat down beside her and handed her a glass of red wine.

'Wonderful,' Annabel said. 'You can keep the bright lights and your clubs and bars, this is so much better. Thank you so much for letting me see it. Oh, look, look,' she squealed. 'Look, there's some ducks and their young.'

'OK, OK,' Rory said. 'Calm down, don't spill your wine. There's only half a bottle left!'

But Annabel leaped to her feet and perched excitedly at the edge of the bank. Afterwards, she was never exactly sure what happened. Did she lose her footing first, or was it that she somehow managed to snap the stem of her glass through sheer excitement, then in looking to see what she'd done, overbalanced? Either way, the outcome was the same.

One foot slid down the side of the bank and Annabel found herself flapping her arms about wildly as she struggled to remain upright and keep the wine in her glass from spilling. Rory just stood there with his mouth open. At the end of it all there was a splash and a scream and Annabel got very wet!

Almost immediately, she found that

the pretty, glinting, bubbling water, although not very deep, was extremely cold. For a brief moment she sat there so shocked by the temperature of the water that her vocal cords were paralysed. Then she found that some reflex had made her hold her glass aloft, with its half stem, in order to prevent it spilling. How crazy could she get? Then she became aware of a sound like a parrot being strangled.

I shall kill him, she thought, and it will be a slow, painful death.

She was thoroughly shaken up, was feeling more than a little foolish and she was icy, icy cold. She did not feel like being laughed at. Rory was on his feet, hovering at the bank's edge but he couldn't keep the amusement out of his eyes.

'I wish you'd control your enthusiasm, Annabel. You've gone and frightened the ducks.'

Annabel shot him a look.

'Are you OK?' he managed in a more serious tone. 'I should have warned you the bank was slippery.'

Annabel stared at her arm, ending with the hand still holding the half full glass of wine. It was the only part of her anatomy that was still dry.

'Shame to waste your precious wine. Cheers!' she said and gulped down the contents with what she hoped was cool aplomb.

'You'd better get out of there. It must be absolutely freezing.'

'Oh, no,' Annabel replied through chattering teeth. 'Quite warm for this time of year. I enjoy the odd dip now and then.'

'Hang on,' Rory said with sudden concern. 'Your hand's bleeding. Come on, let's get you out of there.'

Sure enough, the hand still clutching the wine glass with the broken stem had a trickle of blood oozing from a cut on her forefinger. Not bothering to attempt to keep dry, Rory took two steps down the bank and stood up to mid-calf in the fast-moving water. He took the glass from her hand, stretched over and placed it on the bank, then lifted her carefully to her feet.

By now, the chill and the humiliation of the situation had combined to turn Annabel into a helpless rag doll.

'What an idiot. How did I manage that?' she tried to ask through frozen lips.

'Come on,' Rory said. 'Let's get you inside.'

'I don't think my legs are working.'

'Stop being a drama queen and hold on to me.'

Gratefully, Annabel held on. It was reassuring to have a strong arm to lean on. Her lips had frozen to the extent where her teeth were locked together mid-chatter and her body was so cold and wet, she could hardly move.

'Mustn't forget to come back and get that glass,' Rory said as somehow, he managed to manhandle Annabel up the bank.

'Forget the glass,' Annabel wailed. 'H-how about me? I'm dying of hypothermia here.'

Rory put an arm around her and helped her to manoeuvre her stiff body up through the garden towards his kitchen door.

'The foxes and badgers,' he said shortly. 'Broken glass is dangerous.'

'I kn-kn-know,' Annabel chattered, holding up her bleeding finger. 'Please tell me,' she said a moment later gazing at the small pool of water developing on the flagstones beneath her feet. 'Please t-tell me that this cottage has a hot shower.'

6

Rory's own feet were beginning to feel very uncomfortable, but grateful that at least he hadn't kept his gardening boots on, he bent down and removed his trainers and socks.

'What are you doing?' Annabel asked indignantly as he stooped again to loosen the laces on her boots.

'What d'you think? I'm helping you to get ready for a shower, and, yes, this abode does have a shower and what's more, the water's hot, too.'

'I can do it,' a shivering Annabel said.

'I don't think so,' Rory said in exasperation after watching her struggle with her uncooperative fingers for a few moments.

'All right then, but just the shoes and socks.'

Rory's only answer was a snort of laughter.

'Come on up. I'll turn the shower on for you.'

He raced ahead up the narrow staircase, unsure as to what exactly the state of the bathroom would be. When he got there he heaved a sigh of relief. It was OK, clean, and the towels were hung up over the radiator, not on the floor as he sometimes left them. He glanced round to find Annabel looking very forlorn, standing just inside the door. He turned on the shower and the water came out hot and steamy.

'Right, I'll leave you to it then. Unless you'd like some help, that is,' he added teasingly.

'Actually,' she said in a small voice, 'my fingers are so numb I can't seem to undo anything much.'

'I'll help,' he offered, his hands seeming to find their way with amazing speed to the top button of her shirt. 'No problem.'

Annabel fended him off with her freezing hands and gave him a quelling glance.

'I'm sure you would, but what I was going to say was, I'll just step in there with my clothes on. They're soaking anyway. I'll be able to take them off as soon as my hands warm up.'

'Right,' Rory said. 'Silly of me. Why didn't I think of that?'

'If you could just lend me a bathrobe or something and some trousers and a sweater to go home in.'

'Sure.'

He went to his bedroom and found a strange-looking, never worn, Chinese object his sister had brought him home from Hong Kong, and hung it on the hook behind the bathroom door.

'The towels should be hot enough,' he said. 'I'll put the fire on downstairs and warm the place up a bit.'

What now, Rory wondered when he returned downstairs to the kitchen. Luckily the wood burner was already laid so he put a match to it, then poured himself another glass of wine. He felt he deserved it. He put his soaking trainers outside the back door under the storm porch, then he remembered the glass at the bottom of the garden and went down to fetch it in his bare feet. Then he thought he'd better change his cords, which were clinging round his calves like a couple of wet fish.

He listened carefully outside the bathroom door just to make sure Annabel hadn't fainted or anything, but all he could hear was a bit of splashing. Trying not to feel disappointed because he'd had a short, pleasant fantasy involving him rushing to find her naked on the tiles and then having to give her the kiss of life, he quickly changed into some comfortable jeans. After a little thought, because most of his clothes would be 'way too big for Annabel, he found a reasonable pair of combat pants with a drawstring waist, his best T-shirt and a thick fleece. Then he came down the stairs again and looked in the fridge.

Apart from a few beers, a bag of lettuce and some bacon, there was not a lot going on in there. Never mind, he knew he had a bag of dried pasta that wasn't too far out of date and a bottle of pasta sauce so that should be OK.

That settled, he sat down with his wine and allowed himself to realise that this was really happening. The delectable Annabel was actually in his bathroom, undressed by now, showering with his soap, drying herself on his towels! Rory's strong fingers felt his jaw. He needed a shave. Now, why was he thinking about that? He was getting 'way too far ahead of the game.

Truth to tell, by now, Annabel probably very nearly hated him. Replaying the whole of the scene by the stream again in his mind, Rory winced. He really shouldn't have laughed. He had difficulty suppressing another grin at the memory of Annabel, arms flailing like a windmill, struggling to keep her balance, then landing in such an undignified manner on her rear, right in the middle of the stream.

She'd been such a good sport about

it, too. No hysterics, no screaming or shouting, well, maybe a tiny feminine shriek, as she'd hit the icy cold water. She'd even had the decency not to waste the wine. You had to admire her — what a girl.

Well, he'd have to make it up to her. Be nice, no, be charming. There was a creak on the stairs. He looked round to see Annabel totally swamped by black Chinese dragons on a red background.

'Well, I must say,' Rory said smiling, 'that robe does a lot more for you than it ever did for me. Come and sit by the wood burner. You're probably still cold. Have some more wine. It'll warm you up. After all you . . . '

'Haven't got much on,' Annabel finished for him. 'I know, I've hung my clothes over your bath. I'll stick them in a plastic carrier to take home later. Did you find me some clothes to wear home?'

'I did, yes. They're upstairs, but finish your wine first and warm up a bit. Then while you're changing I'll do some pasta, OK?'

Even to Rory the invitation didn't sound too appealing, but to his surprise Annabel took the glass and sat down right next to the wood burner, warming herself in its blaze.

'I'm such an idiot,' she said. 'I still haven't worked out what happened.'

'No, you're not. You just lost your footing, that's all. It could happen to anyone.'

Rory busied himself around the cooker, fixing a green salad, boiling water for the pasta and frying some chopped bacon to add to the bottle sauce.

'Wow, that was tasty,' Annabel said later.

Much to Rory's amazement, she was still wearing the Chinese robe and what was more, seemed to be in no hurry to get changed and leave. She'd made short work of the pasta, too, and the plate of cheese and biscuits, which was the nearest he could get to a dessert.

The thing was, it was just so easy, so relaxing sitting here together, sharing a glass of wine, talking, laughing, discussing everything under the sun. To his surprise, he'd found himself swapping stories with her about childhood holidays spent with his grandparents in Ayrshire, and she in turn had told him about her rather lonely time as a child but how much she loved the school she'd attended.

'I rather thought you'd have been shipped off to boarding school, you know, jolly hockey sticks and all that.'

'Not at all,' Annabel replied, her face pink and her eyes brighter than usual. 'My dad wanted me near him, so I went to a day school nearby. And before you ask, yes, it was private and, yes, I do know that I was very privileged and very lucky. Also, I play a mean game of hockey. That's how come I'm so good with a spade.'

Rory grinned. He'd asked for that. Much to his relief Annabel smiled back. He'd thought for a moment he'd put his foot in it and she'd taken offence again, but realised that maybe her glowing face was more to do with the wine.

'Everything set for the live afternoon show on Saturday?'

It was the build up to Chelsea, and a programme was being transmitted from a typical small Gloucestershire village show, depicting what went on behind the scenes and how it was organised. With Zoe's assistance, Annabel was covering Highchurch Hill Village Show. It would be live television at its most exciting, the kind of television where you had to think on your feet, and that he knew she most enjoyed.

Annabel drained her glass.

'Yes, I'm really looking forward to it.'

'Not nervous then?'

'Not really.'

Suddenly, he noticed that outside, the light was fading and still they were sitting at his old kitchen table, with Annabel a little on the tipsy side. It was crazy, bizarre, wonderful.

'Why are you staring at me like that?' she asked.

Hastily, Rory changed his expression from what he feared might be lust to that of charming host anxious only for his guest's well-being.

'Who me? Staring? Sorry, didn't mean to. Would you like some more wine? No, maybe better not.'

Annabel looked at her wine glass and seemed to have trouble focusing.

'Think I've probably had enough. Just finish this. Better get my clothes on.'

'You'd better have some coffee,' Rory said.

'You're right. The whole episode on top of a hectic day has hit me. I'm so tired.'

Two cups of strong coffee later, Rory was becoming anxious. Annabel leaned her head on her hands just as her elbow slipped from the table, her head landing on the pine with a thud. Gently, Rory lifted her head from the table.

'I shouldn't have taken that wine. I feel quite tipsy.'

'You're OK. You'll be fine.'

Rory pulled her to her feet and supported her through to the sitting-room. He lowered her cautiously down on to the sofa.

'I can't stay here. What am I gonna do?'

'I suppose a bit of gentle seduction would be out of the question?'

Annabel grinned.

'You're much too nice for that.'

Rory looked down at her lovely face, her soft, inviting lips.

'Am I?'

'Anyway, you're my boss.'

'Yes, yes. Of course I am.'

'You really are rather sweet though.'

Annabel picked up his hand and intertwined their fingers. She giggled and turned on her side. A moment later and she was snoring gently.

7

Annabel stirred, and attempted to remove a strand of hair from her lips. She was aware that her mouth felt rather dry. Slowly she opened her eyes then, as the events of the previous evening came back to her in glorious colour, shut them again.

Keeping her lids closed tightly she listened intently, trying to ascertain Rory's whereabouts. It sounded as though he was in the kitchen and what was more, he was singing. What did that mean? Gingerly, she pushed the blue duvet that was covering her to one side. At least she was still wearing the awful Chinese robe Rory had lent her last night. She wrapped it more firmly round her and rather cautiously made her way up the stairs to the bathroom.

After a shower and rinsing her mouth with mouthwash, she felt a little more human. Gratefully, she retrieved her underwear from the radiator where she'd put it to dry yesterday, then she took a deep breath, tied the robe very tightly round her waist and opened the bathroom door. Just outside were her jeans and shirt, neatly tumble dried and folded. For some inexplicable reason Annabel felt like crying.

Five minutes later, feeling very ill at ease, she was hovering in the kitchen doorway watching Rory, who looked devastatingly handsome as he stirred something in a black pot. He glanced towards her.

'Hi,' he said, as though it were the most natural thing in the world for her to be standing in his kitchen at this time in the morning.

'Good morning,' Annabel said formally. 'Sorry about last night. If I could just have a cup of coffee, I'll be on my way.'

Rory's hair was still damp. He pushed it out of his eyes with the back of his hand.

'Sit down,' he ordered. 'I'm making you some porridge. How d'you want it? I have mine with salt, but some have sugar, or maybe maple syrup.'

'Sugar, please,' Annabel said meekly. 'Really, Rory, I am sorry about last night. I don't know what came over me. I obviously had far too much to drink. Please don't think I make a habit of it.'

'Pleasant though it is to have you grovelling a little, just forget it, eh?'

Rory reached up to a shelf for two blue bowls.

'My fault anyway, as much as yours. Too much wine in the sauce. I was trying to impress you with my skills in the kitchen. Now eat up your porridge like a good girl.'

He handed her a bowl. It didn't look very appetising. Cautiously, she raised her eyes to his and was surprised to find his expression very serious.

'By the way,' he said in a low voice, 'thanks for sticking up for me when Lawrence went in for his character assassination. I meant to tell you last night how much I appreciated it.'

After that, Annabel felt she had to at least attempt the porridge. Manfully she struggled through it, then looked at her watch and with a casual, 'See you later,' beat a hasty retreat.

Up until she reached a familiar road, she was too busy concentrating on Rory's instructions to think in depth about the events of the previous evening. When she did think about it, her face burned with shame. Whatever must he think of her? Drinking that amount surely must have read as an invitation for seduction, dressed, or rather undressed, as she was in that flimsy silk robe. Most men would have taken her up on it, too, or at least kissed her, but he hadn't, had he?

Suddenly, Annabel, instead of feeling grateful that he hadn't, was wondering why. He'd kissed her that once. She felt a delicious shiver shoot down her spine at the memory. Had he found he didn't like it? She didn't turn him on. That was what it was. What other explanation could there be? Annabel found she was driving towards the day's shoot, not only with yesterday's clothes on but also with scalding hot tears pouring down her cheeks.

Contrary to Annabel's expectations the day's shoot went like clockwork, but on reaching home eventually she still gave a sigh of relief.

She'd hardly set eyes on Rory all day. He'd been busy in the vegetable garden, while Annabel and Emma had been filmed admiring the irises and then joined Zoe who was working on a water feature.

'Rory's getting a lot of exposure,' Zoe said at the end of the shoot.

'Is he?' Annabel replied rather abruptly.

Zoe contemplated her through thick black lashes.

'I should say so, yes. I mean we all know he's the star of the show and the female, middle-aged gardener's dream of heaven, but well, you deserve a chance.'

'Oh, I have chances,' Annabel answered,

not sure what Zoe was getting at. 'The live broadcast you and I are doing on Saturday, for a start.'

Zoe snorted.

'I mean real chances. It's common knowledge you didn't get on too well with Rory at first, and well, let's face it, your chance with Beardsley Grange only came up because Lawrence more or less insisted. If Rory had had his way you wouldn't have had a sniff at it.'

'Is that so?'

Annabel's voice sounded cool even to her own ears. Zoe's eyes widened and she took a backward step.

'I haven't put my foot in it, have I? I mean, you and Lawrence — there's nothing going on, is there?'

'Certainly not. Be very sure, there's absolutely nothing going on there. We're passing acquaintances. That's all there is to it.'

'That's what I thought,' Zoe said, a note of satisfaction in her voice.

It wasn't till later that evening, as Annabel was packing an overnight bag for herself, that she wondered why on earth Zoe should want to know the extent of her relationship with Lawrence.

Well, at least she had a day's break with her father to look forward to before going on to Highchurch Hill where she was to film live at Saturday's show. She should be putting all thoughts of work and in particular Rory, out of her mind. Firmly she zipped up her bag and vowed to do just that.

The day's break was taken up with lunch with her father and a couple of his friends so it wasn't until later that afternoon that they were alone and her father mentioned Rory. The two of them were walking in companionable silence along by the herbaceous border.

'You do well together,' Richard said. 'Sebastian was right, Rory was good on his own but the feminine touch softens up the programme. What's he like to work with?'

'Who?'

Richard Grainger's eyes crinkled with amusement.

'The person whose name you've been very careful not to mention.'

'Oh, I suppose you mean Rory Oakhurst.' Her tone was casual, but she bent to sniff at a rose and didn't meet her father's glance. 'Well, I can't say I took to him at first. He can be quite aggressive, bit of a perfectionist, but it's turned out he's OK as it happens. The rest of the team worships him.'

'Do they indeed? And how about you? Do you worship him?'

Annabel made a sound halfway between a laugh and a snort. 'Don't be ridiculous, Dad.'

'Just wondered.'

'I'm really excited about Saturday's project,' Annabel went on hurriedly. 'It's a live broadcast, quite unusual for a gardening show, and it's not very much air time, but I miss the live interviews and I've always been pretty good at them. I don't want to lose my touch.'

'Won't you even have an autocue?'

'Only for the introduction. From then on in, I'll be racing about with a microphone. It'll be fun.'

'When is it on?'

'Saturday, of course. I told you it was live.'

'And will Rory Oakhurst be there?'

'No, he won't. He's doing the build-up to Chelsea. It's just Zoe and I this time.'

Annabel walked stiffly ahead of her father back towards the house. She'd just realised how much she was going to miss Rory over the next couple of days.

★ ★ ★

It was Saturday, it was showtime and, true to form, it was raining. Annabel sat hunched over a rickety table working on her introduction, which she was to read from the autocue before spending her remaining time interviewing visitors to the show.

'How's it going?'

Zoe looked as bedraggled as Annabel

felt. Her hair had started to frizz out of its normal straight style and her thick mascara had smudged.

'OK,' Annabel answered, 'but this isn't as much fun as I thought. Oh, well, at least the viewers will know it's genuine live TV. No-one would plan this little lot.' She pulled a face at the rain sheeting down outside the marquee. 'Your stuff all prepared?'

Zoe was to be stationed in close proximity to various vegetable exhibits ready for Annabel to pounce on during her run-around interviews.

'Yep, I'm all prepared.' She looked at her watch. 'I'd better get cracking. We haven't got long.'

She looked back at Annabel's autocue work.

'You're cutting it a bit fine.'

'Right, I'd better get on with it then.'

Annabel's head went back down over her work. Two minutes later, it was finished, ready for the autocue. Great! Annabel knew she had a really good opening.

'Annabel Grainger?'

A small mousy woman dressed in an overlarge waterproof jacket stood at Annabel's shoulder.

'That's me,' Annabel admitted, checking her lipstick and hair in a small hand mirror.

'There's an urgent message for you at the entrance of the flower arrangers' tent. Someone called Rory.'

Annabel checked her watch. She had ten minutes before she was on air. The introduction was only two minutes. She could see the flower arrangers' tent from where she stood and could be over there and back in no time.

'Thanks,' she said to the departing woman's back.

Of course, she knew Rory wouldn't actually be there in person, but that didn't stop her heart beating at a faster rate than normal. Anxiously, Annabel looked at the sky. The sun was just beginning to show itself at the edge of a bruised-looking cloud and the drizzle had all but stopped. Things were looking up.

The two rain-coated ladies seated at the tent's entrance were busy selling raffle tickets. Trying not to show her impatience, Annabel waited until tickets had been issued and change given.

'I understand there's a message for me. I'm Annabel Grainger.'

She was met by a blank stare, then the one in the blue raincoat suddenly smiled.

'Yes, that's right. An envelope came this morning. I thought one of your lot had already picked it up for you but hang on a moment, I'll check.'

After a few moments searching, the lady appeared with an envelope.

'Here we are,' she said to Annabel.

By now rather anxious that the film crew would be panicking about her whereabouts, Annabel took the envelope and hurried back to the film unit.

'Sorry,' she panted.

'Everything's set,' the sound engineer told her.

Annabel glanced quickly at the autocue. Her opening was up there all ready to roll.

'Fine,' she said, tearing at the envelope.

Inside was a card depicting a rather sketchily-drawn watering can and a bunch of carrots. Annabel opened it up. *Good luck, Rory*, the message read.

OK, fine. That was nice of him. So why did she feel slightly let down? He'd thought of her, which was great, but she would have really liked it if he'd put maybe, *Love from Rory*, or *Thinking of you — always, Rory*, or *Missing you*. That would have been better. *Missing you* said it all.

'Annabel?'

'Yes, OK, I'm ready.'

Butterflies in the stomach, another quick check in the mirror. Countdown time. The autocue started rolling.

'Good afternoon,' Annabel started. 'Well, unfortunately, the weather here at Highchurch Hill hasn't quite come up to expectations but, well, what's a little drizzle between friends? The residents of Highchurch Hill are not only friendly, they're generous, too.'

Annabel faltered a little. Something was wrong. Her copy, although it was hers, wasn't reading like hers. The punctuation had started to go haywire.

'Because although this show appears to be typical of many . . . other village shows happening up and down the country. Even as we speak, the people of Highchurch Hill are . . . contributing all their profits to charity. The show consists of the village hall and two marquees, one full to bursting . . . with arts and crafts, one concentrating on fresh produce, locally grown.'

By now, Annabel was red in the face and stuttering. What on earth was going on? She always punctuated her copy meticulously, allowing for gaps in the dialogue in order to draw breath, marking where she was to move along and start her interviewing. Something had clearly gone very wrong, and it was live. No-one could shout, 'Cut,' so she could have another attempt.

Annabel smiled into the camera.

'Well, it appears something has gone wrong with my autocue, but we won't worry about that, will we? Let's just get on with the interviewing and let the marvellous people of Highchurch Hill tell their own story.'

'It was so unprofessional, so embarrassing,' Annabel wailed later. 'I'll have nightmares about it for the rest of my life.'

'Don't worry,' Zoe soothed. 'It could happen to anyone.'

'No, it couldn't. At the moment, with my luck, it could only happen to me. I can't, just can't understand it. My copy was fine. You saw me doing it. I'd checked it through at least half a dozen times. It was perfect. Then I got that stupid message from Rory and by the time I got back, everything was ready to go, and anyway, it was right, I knew it was right. I just don't understand it,' she finished dismally.

Zoe pushed a cup of steaming tea into Annabel's hand.

'Look, stop torturing yourself. These things happen. Give yourself a break. Most of the viewers won't have noticed and those who did probably thought, at least it proves it's live TV, not yet another recorded show.'

But Annabel was not to be pacified.

'I'll never live it down,' she said, putting her head in her hands. 'And what will Rory think? What will he say? He'll crucify me.'

'Well, if you ask me, it was partly his fault.'

'How?' Annabel asked. 'How can it possibly be his fault?'

'Well, he sent you the stupid message, didn't he? And what was so urgent about saying no more than *Good Luck*, I wonder.'

Annabel blinked.

'No, it was my fault. I shouldn't have been so unprofessional as to leave my post like that at the last minute. I wouldn't tolerate it from anyone else and I shouldn't have done it. It's got nothing to do with Rory.'

Zoe heaved a large sigh as Annabel looked at her with a question mark in her eyes.

'What?'

Shrugging her shoulders, Zoe dropped her eyes.

'I really hoped you'd be immune.'

'What d'you mean?'

'You know what I mean. Another conquest for Rory Oakhurst. No woman is safe.'

Annabel felt herself flushing.

'You talk as though you have personal experience,' she said, hating herself for wanting to hear more, yet unable to turn away.

'Oh, yes, I have personal experience all right. Never lasts long, though. He's a 'love-them-and-leave-them' kind of guy. Likes the chase, you know. Once he catches you, well, you know the story. Happens all the time.'

There was a long silence.

'I see,' Annabel said eventually. 'Well,

I suppose I should say thanks for warning me, but I'd already decided business and pleasure don't mix, so nothing has happened, and nothing will happen between Rory and me. Anyway,' she ended, 'Rory really doesn't go for me. I'm not his type.'

8

Rory was in a quandary. He'd heard about Annabel's sudden inability to read her own copy from the autocue and even though he felt a stirring of sympathy, his overriding emotion was one of annoyance. He'd always known she was overconfident. It was to do with her background, Daddy always telling her she could do everything, leaving university with a string of high qualifications. No wonder she thought she could do anything and everything with her hands tied behind her back.

He thought back to the night she'd stayed when he had mentioned the coming live broadcast to her. She had said it would be easy, peasy! His expression softened for a moment as he remembered Annabel, deliciously tipsy, clad only in the Chinese robe and a silly smile, then his face darkened. It was no good. He had to have a word with her. She'd been sloppy; she must have been. No television journalist worth their salt would leave copy, about to go on autocue, unattended, or not check it immediately prior to the broadcast.

Having decided this, he cast around in his mind for excuses. The weather was bad, that was always off-putting. People were pushing and shoving all around, struggling to get in from the rain. Some of the technical team were new, and she'd had only a minimal team anyway. But the fact remained that whereas Zoe had come across as friendly, natural and knowledgeable where it mattered, Annabel, although she had made a good recovery, had clearly been wrong-footed at the start.

The thing to do was just play this as though she was someone else, Zoe for instance. He would say to Zoe that her opening was a bit of a shambles. What happened? Rory smiled with relief. Yes, that was how he'd tackle it. A reprimand, but not too serious. Play it by ear, give her a chance to put her side then, after making it clear that, while she was a representative of **Dig Your Garden**, he didn't expect it to happen again, things would go back to normal. And what exactly was normal, he wondered to himself. Was all this, not being able to wait to see her again, was this normal? And all this mooning about when it was Chelsea week and he should be working his socks off, was this normal, too?

I really must get Annabel out of my system, he told himself, treat her like a colleague, the same way I treat Zoe. He decided to speak to her privately at the show garden before the filming for the weekly show. It was a situation he would normally deal with easily and lightly. No need to make a big deal about it, no need at all, but he was undeniably nervous and it was with a set expression that he finally faced Annabel for the first time since the broadcast.

''Morning.'

''Morning,' Annabel answered in subdued tones. 'Sorry I messed up.'

She'd taken away his thunder. Now what could he say?

'Well, the opening was a bit of a shambles,' Rory said, struggling to get back to his planned script. 'What happened?'

'Don't know,' Annabel admitted. 'When I left my copy, it was perfect. When I came back there wasn't time for any checking and I had no reason to believe it wasn't still fine, but once we were on air, I couldn't read it properly. The punctuation was all over the place so it didn't make sense. I just don't understand what went wrong.'

'Well, what was so important that you had to rush off at the last minute?'

Immediately he'd finished speaking, Rory realised what an insensitive question that was.

'Never mind,' he said. 'It's none of my business and it really doesn't make any difference.'

Annabel looked crestfallen. Once

upon a time he knew he'd have been delighted to see her expression of defeat, but now he felt as though he'd stuck a knife in her back.

'No need to look so stricken. I'm just disappointed, that's all.'

And it was true, he recognised, he was disappointed. But he'd no right to be. He'd put Annabel on a pedestal, and that was why he'd expected perfection.

'It's all right,' he went on in a gentler tone. 'I'm not going to fire you. Even if I were of a mind to, I'm sure Sebastian wouldn't hear of it.'

There was a long silence, then Annabel stuck her chin out and glared at him in defiance.

'He doesn't have to hear of it. I'm resigning.'

This was going all wrong. Rory stared in disbelief at Annabel's sudden flushed face and stubborn expression.

'What?'

'You heard me quite clearly. I've been thinking about it and it's the obvious thing to do.'

Rory sat down on the nearest chair.

'Oh, Annabel, don't be silly. I haven't got time for this. And you know I really don't want you to leave.'

'It's not about what you want. It's about what I want and I don't want the aggravation of your continual insinuations that I'm only here because my father happens to know Sebastian, that I haven't a vestige of talent and I'm not good at my job. I can do without that, thank you very much.'

Rory stared at her fiery expression, and the angry tilt of her chin. Her lips were trembling. Rory stared in fascination, aware that more than anything in the world he wanted to kiss them, taste their sweetness.

Get a grip, Oakhurst, you can't kiss her now, not while she's making a speech of resignation.

'Annabel, sit down. You know I don't think any of those things.'

'I don't want to sit down. My contract was only for three months anyway. I won't be expecting a renewal.

I'll finish the research I started for a couple more projects and you can get someone else decorative to fill the gap. That shouldn't be too difficult for someone like you. There's Zoe, for instance. She's very attractive in an obvious kind of way. She'd be a good choice. Maybe for old times' sake? I understand you've been much more than just good friends.'

Completely baffled, Rory continued to stare at her. She'd worked herself up into a fury. Why? What had he said? It almost sounded as though she was angry with him for having Zoe as a friend. Angry with him, because of Zoe? Wearily, Rory shook his head.

'Annabel,' he started, 'you're too hard for me. Too difficult for me to understand.'

Annabel's eyes flashed fire.

'Good,' she said, 'because the last person I want to be understood by is you, Rory Oakhurst. Got that?'

She stormed off and set to work, in an attempt to calm her thoughts.

Some time later, in a corner of the show garden Annabel dug furiously. Strictly speaking, she didn't have to dig, but she felt like it.

'Want some tea?' a voice interrupted her thoughts.

Annabel glanced round with a barely concealed glare, then her expression softened.

'Thanks, Emma, that's kind.'

Emma sat down on the turf next to her.

'What are you doing?'

'Digging,' Annabel replied shortly.

Emma picked a blade of grass.

'Look, don't take this wrong but, don't be so hard on Rory. He's a good bloke.'

'Huh!'

Emma tried again.

'I know you haven't seen him exactly at his best and I heard Zoe saying to you that he hadn't given you chances, but it's not true. He gave Colin his chance and me mine. He's good at his job and he's very loyal. I know sometimes he's a bit brusque, but he doesn't mean it. He won't hear a word against you, you know. Thinks you're a trouper and a real professional.'

Annabel watched as Emma shredded the blade of grass into fine ribbons of green.

'Thanks, Emma,' she said. 'I appreciate your concern, but it isn't working and that's all there is to it.'

Emma got to her feet.

'I have to go, but I really hope you'll change your mind.'

Annabel looked up.

'About what?'

'About leaving, of course.'

'Hang on a moment. Who said I was leaving?'

An uneasy expression passed across Emma's face.

'Well, Zoe said . . . '

'Oh, did she?'

'Aren't you then?'

'I suppose I am.'

After Emma had left the garden where she was working, Annabel sat and thought. What was the matter with her? Where was her normal cool, calm self? Why did she have to overreact every time Rory was in the vicinity?

And how come Rory had spread the news straightaway and spoken to Zoe of all people? Couldn't wait to get rid of her obviously. Come to think of it, Zoe professed to know an awful lot about everything going on at **Dig Your Garden**, an awful lot about just about everything now she had time to consider.

Thoughtfully, Annabel picked up the border fork and slowly but methodically started to break up the soil and remove the spent blooms. She thought back to the Highchurch Hill broadcast and the autocue business. Zoe had been hanging round as she'd finished her opening, then she'd got the message from the small, mousy lady to go to the flower arrangers' tent. Had Zoe been there then?

No, Annabel was almost sure she'd just left to take up her position by the vegetable exhibits, but afterwards, when Annabel had struggled to find out what could have gone wrong with her copy, she remembered the sound engineer saying that no-one who shouldn't have been there had gone anywhere near the autocue.

Annabel stopped with her fork in mid air. But if Zoe had been there, the sound engineer wouldn't have thought twice about it, would he? It would have taken Zoe less than two minutes to alter the punctuation randomly, then run back round to her own position. And when Annabel had gone to pick up her message, what had the lady in the blue Macintosh said?

'Oh, I thought one of your lot had picked it up earlier.'

So suppose Zoe had picked up Rory's card and hung on to it until five minutes before airtime? She could easily have asked the mousy lady to deliver the line about an urgent message from Rory. She'd probably worked out by now that any message from Rory would be important to Annabel, more important than it should be, too. Yes, it could have happened that way, but why?

Surely Zoe didn't want the job that badly? And she'd been so sympathetic afterwards, too.

Systematically, Annabel went over all the conversation Zoe had had with her. The only one that really stuck out in her mind was when she had hinted that Annabel had fallen for Rory and that Rory would drop her like a hot brick once he'd had his way with her, and fool that she was, Annabel had half believed it.

What an idiot! She'd let Zoe get to her and the very next conversation she'd had with Rory she'd wound herself up, pretended to herself that the reason for her fury was because Rory had dared criticise her work, which after all, was criticism well justified. But, if she were honest, the real reason for her emotional outburst was Zoe's intimation that she and

Rory had been an item and he'd treated her badly. She was jealous, that was what all this was about.

Where Rory was concerned she, Annabel Grainger, was jealous of anyone and everyone and Zoe was playing on that jealousy to do Annabel out of a job.

Well, Zoe, it isn't over yet, she thought to herself. I still have three weeks of my contract to run and I'll be watching you every step of the way.

★ ★ ★

On the whole, if it weren't for a certain coolness between Annabel and himself, Rory was fairly content with life. He was in control again, he thought. Despite the rather strange scene with Annabel, things seemed to have simmered down, on the work front anyway. Annabel, polite and slightly distant, had either decided to work out her contract, or was treating the exchange where she'd given her notice in as never having happened. He wasn't sure which.

If he missed the occasional heated difference of opinion he'd come to expect and half enjoy, the fact that she was still around and therefore open to persuasion to renew her contract, more than made up for it.

Of course, he still indulged in ridiculous daydreams of a rather passionate nature, but for now, with Chelsea week over and praise and acclaim coming from all sides, Rory was content to let sleeping Annabels lie and start work on the many new openings his exposure from Chelsea had brought about.

He'd had a tempting proposition from a publisher to consider, as well as a ten-minute spot featuring gardening for the elderly, on an early evening programme.

This is your time, Oakhurst, he told himself. Make sure you make the most of it.

★ ★ ★

It was the first week in June when Sebastian and Rory met up for lunch. Although slightly resenting the amount of power a producer of Sebastian's stature wielded, Rory had none the less built up a healthy respect for him.

He dressed carefully in a light linen suit and a blue shirt. It didn't take him long to decide on a tie because he only had two and one of those was black. But he took care to arrive at the restaurant punctually. He knew Sebastian's little foibles.

Sebastian, when he arrived, was full of compliments, but not above reminding him that hiring Annabel was his idea.

'Great girl,' he said. 'Brains, beauty, charm, she's got the lot, that one. Whoever ends up marrying her will be a lucky man, eh?'

'Yes indeed,' Rory said.

'The Beardsley Grange programme will become a classic,' Sebastian went on. 'The chemistry between those two

136

was marvellous, didn't you think?'

'Yes, indeed,' Rory said again.

'The last interview in the fernery was just exquisite. Excellent stuff, wouldn't you say?'

'Yes, excellent,' Rory agreed. 'Colin's photography was superb.'

'Well, yes, that, too,' Sebastian conceded.

They ordered their meals then, and went on to talk of the viewing figures and those of their nearest rivals.

'You know, Oakhurst,' Sebastian said and leaned forward conspiratorially, 'I think we could topple them. If we brought Lawrence Beardsley in and, whisper has it, he fancies himself as some kind of a media host, well, we both know he's hardly that, but with the right props around him and someone who knows the ropes, like Annabel, he could make for controversial and compulsive viewing.'

Dumbfounded and trying not to show it, Rory cast around desperately for something to say.

'There's a lot on our team already,' he started.

'He wouldn't be on the team, Oakhurst. Just guesting fairly regularly, that's all. He's a personality, you see, a character, and the viewers love them. It's a shame you didn't hit it off with him, but, still, he doesn't hit it off with any man over five foot ten. Gives him a complex. Ghastly bloke, but looks good on the box. There you have it. You needn't have much to do with him. You'll still be our resident host, it goes without saying, but you've other irons in the fire now and actually the contrast between you both is rather good.'

The silence this time went on for longer than Rory could bear.

'Certainly worth consideration,' he said eventually.

9

Over the next week, Annabel made sure that whenever Zoe was around, her own manner towards Rory was cool, bordering on the icy. With Zoe herself, Annabel tried to keep the relationship much as it had always been, casual but friendly.

Any overtures towards a warmer level of friendship she left to Zoe, and sure enough, her patience was rewarded. Zoe made more and more excuses to appear by Annabel's side and feed her titbits of information, all designed to discredit Rory in Annabel's eyes.

The only time Zoe did insist on some privacy, Annabel noticed, was when certain calls came through on her mobile. Then, if Annabel were in the vicinity, Zoe would lower her voice and wander away. A couple times it crossed Annabel's mind that it could be Rory on the other end of the line, and that Zoe was playing a double game of some kind, but that theory was scotched when, in the middle of one of these intimate conversations, conducted in a low tone just out of earshot, Rory walked in demanding to know where everyone was. Annabel itched to know who the mystery person was and what such an obviously private conversation was about.

One morning, during the last shot of the session, Rory, Emma and Annabel were in what was referred to as the dry garden. This was one of Annabel's favourite areas of the show garden. With only a number of large, rocky outcrops and sparse, sandy soil to sustain it, the plants used there had to do without water for the whole year. She loved the way that with very little encouragement the grey-leafed, sun-loving plants could thrive on next to nothing.

Some of the planting had got a little out of hand, and some had seeded themselves in unlikely places, so Rory was commenting on these occurrences with Emma chiming in with questions. Watching from the sidelines until her part came up, Annabel tried not to stare at Rory too openly, but it was difficult. As usual he was dressed in comfortable old jeans and a very ordinary blue shirt, but Annabel had to admit that with his lean and athletic build he made a striking figure.

Rory completed his sequence in the way Annabel had come to expect, professionally and with an effortless charm, as though he were talking to one person, not millions. The smile he gave as he used the line to link to the next shot was wide and genuine and caused Annabel's heart to lurch.

When his filming was completed, Rory told Emma she could go, but hung on to watch Annabel's final shot of the morning, which involved the brutal lopping of various Mediterranean-type perennials whilst she informed the viewers that this would ensure further flowering later in the year.

'Well done,' he said when she'd finished.

She could see it was his intention to help her down the narrow, gravel path with her tools and wasn't sure she could trust herself to be so close to him. In order to allow her to pass, he stood to one side but, reluctant to let him too near, she backed away then gave a strangled cry as her arm caught against the razor sharp spear of a yucca plant.

'Oh, no,' Rory said, 'not again. Any time I come anywhere near, you end up having some kind of an accident. Please tell me it wasn't my fault.'

Annabel looked into his eyes for a long moment. The air in the small distance between them was electric. His eyes shone against his wind-burned features and Annabel would have given anything in the world to have been able to run a finger along the line of his wide, humorous mouth and his square jaw.

His eyes were the first to drop.

'Here, let me look at that.'

The touch of his fingers scorched her skin. She took a shuddering breath.

'It wasn't your fault, but,' she said as she pulled her arm away, 'I think I'd better get this washed.'

Rory appeared to have been turned to stone. Rather than try to read his expression, she dropped her secateurs, gloves and small garden fork on the path, then turned and hurried away from him.

Five minutes later, she stood quietly inside a cubicle of the ladies washroom. She'd washed what had proved to be only a surface scratch on her arm, and was now busily engaged in drying her eyes, telling herself to cease the snivelling, which had nothing to do with her arm, and buck up.

The outside door to the Ladies swung open and Annabel recognised Zoe's murmured tones.

'It's got to be tonight,' she was saying quietly into, Annabel guessed, her ever-present mobile phone. 'I know he's going to be alone,' she went on, 'because I just asked him. No, no he'll be in his cottage, licking his wounds. You should see the smouldering, reproachful glances he shoots her. Rory doesn't want a shoulder to cry on. I've tried the sympathy routine, but he doesn't want to know. Best to stick to our plan. I'll just turn up out of the blue with a bottle, a screw-type bottle and I'll make sure he handles it.'

There was silence for a moment during which Annabel found she was holding her breath.

'Well, I don't have to stay, do I? Once he's handled the bottle, and the drink's got the drug in it, it'll be his word against mine. The tabloid Press will love it. Of course, if I can get in the cottage, I will, but don't count on it.'

The person on the other end appeared to be arguing now, because Zoe sighed a couple of times.

'Well, if you think a black eye will help, I'll just bop myself one with a tennis ball. All right, I suppose it's the only way. I just hope you're right about Sebastian letting you step into Rory's shoes, that's all.'

There was further conversation from the other end of the call.

'Oh, I'm confident about that. I should have had the job in the first place, even Rory knows that. Right, fine, yep, I'll meet you at The Red Lion afterwards. I'll call you first. OK, 'bye, Lawrence.'

Lawrence! Although part of Annabel wanted to burst out of the cubicle and confront Zoe, she didn't move a muscle. It wasn't until Zoe had left and a good five minutes had passed that she crept out of the Ladies and over to where Emma was working. The beginning of a plan was forming in Annabel's mind.

'Emma, d'you think Colin would lend me a hand-held movie camera if I promised to take very great care of it?'

Emma looked up.

'Ah, there you are. Zoe was looking

145

for you a minute ago. She said she'll catch you later.'

She thinks she will, no doubt of that, Annabel thought to herself. No doubt at all.

'Well, do you?'

'Oh, the camera? Don't see why not. Going somewhere special then?'

'I might be,' Annabel answered with an enigmatic smile.

★   ★   ★

Rory couldn't wait to get home. He didn't try to fool himself that it was in order to start work on the newly-commissioned book, on gardens past and present, either. The reason he wanted to get home was in order to think long and hard, about his relationship with Annabel.

But, that was just the problem — did he have a relationship with Annabel? Today, up in the dry garden, when all he'd wanted to do was help, she'd shrunk away from him, as though he were contagious. He didn't know if he could carry on working with her, watching her, trying not to notice how beautiful she was, or how sweet her smile was, or how much he'd like to kiss those inviting lips. It was unfair. It was more than he, Rory, could stand.

With images of Annabel never far away, he drove to the cottage on autopilot. At one point, he thought for a crazy moment that Annabel's car was behind him, but he must have imagined it, because there was no sign of it at the next set of traffic lights.

Getting delusional now, Oakhurst, he told himself.

The side of his car brushed against the hawthorn hedge as he pulled up in front of his cottage door. He should really cut it back before it damaged the car. A bit of physical effort would be good for him, but he knew he didn't feel like it. Didn't really feel like doing anything, in fact, apart from indulging in a drink and a shower, in that order.

An hour later, with damp hair and

clean clothes, he sat sprawled on the wooden bench by the stream. He swirled his whisky round in his glass. What had gone so wrong between Annabel and himself, since the evening she'd fallen in the stream, he wondered.

He recognised that on waking next morning and remembering what had happened, she must have felt a bit of a fool, but overindulging in the drinks' department wasn't that serious an offence, surely? It wasn't as if he'd forced her mouth open and poured it down her throat, or forced anything on her for that matter. In fact he'd behaved like a perfect gentleman throughout, something that he sometimes regretted!

He stared dismally at the stream still gurgling along. Wild yellow irises and ragged robin were flowering on the bank. A blackbird was sitting at the top of an elderberry farther down stream, singing his heart out. If only Annabel were here to appreciate the changes that had taken place in just a couple of weeks, if only he had Annabel to share all this with.

There was the sound of an engine dying and then the slam of a car door. For a moment Rory's heart leaped. Perhaps it was Annabel after all. He leaped to his feet, half spilling his whisky in his anxiety to return to the house. Sure enough he could hear the doorbell before he'd entered the kitchen.

'Hang on,' he shouted, his heart beating up in his throat somewhere.

He flung open the door, then felt the smile die on his lips.

'Zoe!'

'That's me,' Zoe replied.

She was holding a bottle of wine, which was shoved immediately into his surprised hands.

'Well, aren't you going to invite me in?'

Oh, no, if there was one thing he didn't need right now, it was this.

'Sorry, Zoe, not tonight, OK? Some other time perhaps.'

He cast around in his mind for an excuse, any excuse.

'Right now, I have to get some kind of outline down on paper for that publisher I told you about.'

Zoe shrugged her shoulders.

'One little drink wouldn't take long. You seemed so down, I thought you needed cheering up.'

'Me, down? Don't know what you mean,' Rory lied. 'Honestly, Zoe, much as I appreciate the thought, I really can't spare the time.'

He pushed the bottle back into her hands, half expecting her not to take it, but not only did she take it, she made no further attempt to get past him.

'Well,' she began doubtfully, 'if you're sure you're all right.'

''Course I'm all right. Don't know what gave you the idea I might not be. I'll probably have a sandwich, then get my head down over the computer. Sorry, Zoe, another time, eh?'

Zoe swung her hair and looked at him from under mascaraed lashes.

'Sure, Rory,' she said. 'I was on my way home anyway, but, well, you can't blame a girl for trying.'

Now what was that supposed to mean? Zoe was a mate. Rory had always been confident that there was nothing of a remotely romantic nature between them. That was why working together was so easy. Now here she was practically propositioning him. He shook his head in bewilderment. Women, you just never knew where you were with them.

Carefully, Zoe placed the wine in the boot then swung her legs into her car. The puzzled expression still on his face, Rory watched until her car had vanished down the lane.

Because he'd mentioned getting down to work on the first rough outline for Gardens Past and Present, Rory decided that that would be precisely what he'd do. So after making himself a thick cheese and pickle sandwich and pouring a beer, he opened his laptop and, resolving to put all thoughts of women in general and Annabel in particular out of his mind, he settled down to work.

Half an hour later, he again heard the sound of a car. Oh, no, not Zoe back again. Reluctantly he opened the door.

'Annabel!'

'Hi,' Annabel said with a dazzling smile. 'Wondered if you'd like to help me finish this.'

She held up an almost empty wine bottle.

What was it with all these women with bottles suddenly throwing themselves at him? Then he looked closer. Annabel's hair was dishevelled, her eyes bright, face flushed. His eyes narrowed.

'How much of that did you drink?'

Annabel looked at him as though it were a trick question.

'All of it, silly,' she said.

'You'd better come in,' he said, 'and you should never have driven here in this state.'

'What state?' Annabel asked innocently. 'Thought you liked a girl who could hold her drink.'

Funny the way her slightly slurred speech seemed to come and go. If he didn't know better, he would almost think she was putting on an act, but why on earth would she do that?

'Have you eaten?' Rory asked. 'I'll make you a sandwich.'

'Rather have a drink.'

'I dare say, but a cheese sandwich is what you'll get, followed by a strong coffee. Then I'll book you a room at The Red Lion and take you there myself.'

Rory bent down and picked up Annabel's heavy bag, then noticed an expensive camera sitting on the top. He pushed it more securely down the side of the bag. Tipsy or not, she wouldn't want to damage that. For a moment Annabel looked panic stricken.

'What's the matter now?' he asked.

She shut the heavy oak door and leaned against it as though she was having trouble standing upright.

153

'I was kind of hoping I might stay here.'

What? What had she just said? Rory ran a hand over his chin. He needed a shave. No! He wasn't going there. With a glint of challenge in her eyes, Annabel continued to stare at him. Resolutely, Rory hardened his heart.

'Now what on earth made that idea pop into your mind? No, don't tell me. The drink, of course. It appears that you only fancy me when you're drunk, but me? I like my women sober. Now, I'll make you that sandwich and some strong, black coffee. You'll feel differently then. This is a non-entertainment evening for me, I'm afraid. I've got work to do, serious work.'

One of the hardest things he'd ever had to do in his life, he thought afterwards, was to walk to the kitchen, fill up the kettle and plug it in, when all he really wanted to do was take the delectable Annabel into his arms and never let her go.

10

The birds' chorus woke Annabel at five-thirty. For the second time in as many weeks, she pushed a plain blue duvet cover from around her shoulders and carefully eased herself from the squeaky sofa. Instead of being in the Chinese robe, however, this time she was in her rather crumpled jeans and T-shirt.

Slowly, she crept up the stairs, avoiding the one second from the bottom, because she'd already noticed its creak. Outside Rory's door, she paused for a second, grinning to herself. A series of gentle snores was just audible through the thick pine door.

Five minutes later, with an open street map next to her, she was driving through the Sussex countryside on her way to where Zoe lived. Who was it who had said surprise was of the essence?

Annabel didn't know, but was banking on it being true.

There had been a couple of heart-stopping moments last night, when she'd really thought that Rory would pick her up and bodily throw her into his car merely in order to get rid of her. She knew she was no actress and playing drunk was, she found, a difficult thing to do. It had helped though, that as soon as she'd finished her sandwich and coffee, Rory had switched on his laptop and totally ignored her.

Easy then to lie on the sofa, breathe steadily and easily, for two hours, or it should have been, but with echoes of Zoe's one-sided conversation buzzing round in her mind, Annabel found it difficult to relax. And when, at what she guessed must be about ten-thirty, Rory had whispered in her ear that really he should take her to The Red Lion to spend the night, she couldn't help but flinch.

'Ah, so you are awake,' he'd said.

Annabel had immediately let her

body go limp, and refused to open her eyes again. Eventually, she heard him clump off up the stairs and return with the duvet, which he seemed to spend a lot of time tucking round her. After that, there had been the clink of china and the sound of the back door being locked, then weary footsteps on the stairs, noises from the bathroom, and finally, silence.

Driving along now, with the early-morning sun just catching the tops of the trees, Annabel grinned to herself and punched the air. The first part of her plan had worked. Now for the second, most difficult, part. She had to confront Zoe!

Zoe lived on the outskirts of Brighton. Emma had been there once and had remembered the name of the road but not the number.

'It's a house divided into two flats,' she had told Annabel. 'It's got two blue doors, Zoe's is the one on the right. But why don't you ask her yourself?'

Annabel swallowed hard. What possible excuse could she give? Curiosity radiated from every pore of Emma's body.

'What's going on?'

'Please, Emma, promise me you won't say anything about this,' she said. 'I promise you I'm not going to murder her or anything like that. It's to do with Rory, to do with the job. I can't explain, but please trust me.'

For a long moment, Annabel held Emma's inquisitive stare.

'Right,' Emma said. 'I promise.'

And now, here was the street. Annabel looked at her watch. Just gone six. She hoped Zoe was not an early riser. Slowly, Annabel travelled down the road. Luckily it was a short road of only about a hundred houses, several of which had been divided into two flats but only one of which had two blue front doors.

As silently as she could, Annabel pulled up round the corner of the street. Remember, the surprise factor.

She took the camera from her bag and locked it in the boot of the car. Then with her bag on her shoulder and taking a deep breath, she walked up to the house and rang the bell of the door on the right. At first there was no answer. Annabel kept herself close to the blue door, and out of sight of any downstairs windows. After a third ring, when she kept her finger on the bell for a prolonged period, there were noises from within.

'OK, OK, I'm coming,' she heard Zoe's voice.

Annabel braced herself. She was counting on Zoe being groggy with sleep and in no physical state to keep Annabel out.

The door opened. Quick as a flash, Annabel was inside.

'Surprise, surprise,' she said.

'Annabel!'

There was amazement tempered with disbelief all over Zoe's face.

'Expecting someone else? Lawrence perhaps?'

Rings of black mascara were round Zoe's eyes, but even so, Annabel could see that one lid was puffy and bloodshot.

'Oh, dear, had an accident with a tennis ball?'

Zoe's mouth dropped open. Annabel marched past her through the tiny hall and into the sitting-room. On the coffee table stood an empty screw-top bottle of wine.

'Ah,' Annabel said, snatching it up. 'Evidence, I presume, Watson?'

'Put that down. What are you doing?' Zoe screeched.

Ignoring her, Annabel walked on through to the kitchen, turned on the tap and started washing the bottle.

'Stopping you from making a fool of yourself, Zoe,' she said over her shoulder.

Zoe sank down on to the nearest chair, and regarded Annabel from her blackened panda eyes.

'Have you gone crazy or something? I don't know what you're on about.'

'Oh, I think you do. I think you know exactly what I'm on about. You've already done a nice little hatchet job on my career, by messing with my copy before it went on autocue, and now you're trying to ruin Rory with some crazy smear about him. I don't know, but were you to accuse him of attacking you, raping you? Something so totally out of character for Rory that nobody would believe you anyway.'

'Why shouldn't they believe me? And anyway, how do you know all this?'

Annabel hesitated. Zoe looked very vulnerable sitting there in her skimpy nightie and with her swollen eye.

'Because I overheard you talking to Lawrence, that's how. Oh, Zoe, how could you? He's such a piece of rubbish. Rory's worth ten of him.'

Zoe sighed, and her shoulders slumped.

'Lawrence wants Rory's job. He wants to be a personality, he wants the fame, and he promised me your job,' Zoe said simply.

'Yes, but, Zoe, what if it backfired? It

was all you, wasn't it? You bought the wine and the drug you doctored it with. You went round to his cottage and got Rory to put his fingerprints on it. You're the one who blacked your own eye, you're the one who'll be making the accusations and signing a false police statement. You've been stupid, Zoe. You're the only one implicated. Lawrence has made sure he is totally in the clear. What's he done, apart from making the bullets and watching you fire them?'

Zoe's face had gone a sickly shade.

'I would never have gone to the police,' she said. 'It was just meant to be a rumour about Rory attacking me, a threat. With his fingerprints on the bottle with the remains of the drugged wine, he wouldn't have a leg to stand on. Any Press coverage would be enough to make Sebastian ask Rory to resign. Sebastian would have been happy enough to see Lawrence in his place. That's why I took my chance with you at the village show. I thought if you'd already gone, I'd stand more chance of getting your job after all the fuss had died down.'

'I see,' Annabel said. 'Well, your story won't stand up now, will it? You weren't the only one at the cottage last night. I was there with Colin's camera, the one that records the time and date, and I have footage of you standing on Rory's doorstep, thrusting the bottle of wine at him in order to get his fingerprints, then getting in your car and driving off. Oh, and after that, I went and knocked on his door, but he didn't turn me away, so I stayed all night, and I'm ready to swear to it in a court of law if necessary.'

Tears were squeezing themselves through Zoe's eyelids.

'Have you told Rory?' she whispered

For a moment Annabel felt sorry for her.

'No,' she said shortly. 'I haven't. I reckon he thinks we're both quite mad. I'll leave you to tell Lawrence that the plan didn't work and I think you might

163

add that it would be as well to refuse any propositions Sebastian might make about his working with either Rory or me in the future.'

'I told Lawrence it was a stupid idea. I must have been crazy to let him talk me into it.'

'I wish you'd talked to me,' Annabel said. 'I've got contacts, and there are other programmes. Anyway, it's better to work your way up slowly. Be reliable, be professional. People who take shortcuts without the experience don't usually last long, but the last thing you need is a lecture from me.'

'What about you?' Zoe asked. 'What will you do?'

'Me? Oh, I'll be fine. I won't renew my contract so you'll probably get my job. I might go back to children's TV. I like the company better.'

Still holding the wine bottle, Annabel left Zoe and walked out of the flat.

Annabel wasn't due at the show garden until the following day when she was to meet up with the team to discuss the next week's filming, and do a walk-through at the various parts of the garden to be featured. So, with a feeling of anti-climax, she drove straight to her London flat and indulged in a long, hot shower. Only when she was freshly changed, with a plate of toast and marmalade in front of her, did she think about what she would say to Rory the next day.

Simply thinking about it brought her out in a cold sweat. Perhaps she could ring him, resign over the phone, but she knew deep down it wasn't an option. She'd have to go in, face the music, and comfort herself with the knowledge that at least she'd saved his reputation.

But whatever did he think of her now? What had he said? He liked his women sober. Surely he must despise her. Probably he never wanted to see her again.

When she arrived at the show garden, she could see Rory's car parked under the shade of the old copper beech. She grabbed the bag containing Colin's camera and made her way inside the house, the bottom part of which acted as offices for the programme. The offices seemed strangely quiet.

'Hi,' she called. 'Anyone here?'

'Yep, me. I'm here.'

Arms folded, Rory strode out from a side room. Annabel's heart sank within her. His face was like a thundercloud. His flint grey eyes glared into hers.

'I want an explanation,' he barked.

Annabel felt slightly scared.

'Why? What have I done? And where is everyone?'

'They're in the canteen,' Rory said. 'I didn't want them to cramp my style.'

'Well, if you're thinking of firing me, I've already quit, remember? So you can stop bullying me. If you don't want me to finish my contract, that suits me fine, too.'

Angry tears were beginning to make themselves felt on her cheeks. Hotly, she dashed them away.

'Now, if you'll just get out of my way,

I have something I have to give back to Colin.'

Rory didn't move.

'Ah, that would be that rather expensive camera you borrowed.'

Momentarily wrong-footed, Annabel paused.

'Oh, well, if you already know about it . . . ' She delved in her bag and brought out the camera. 'You can tell him he can wipe off whatever's on there, it's no longer important.'

A twitch had started at the corner of Rory's lips.

'Who says it's not important? I happen to think it's very important, very important indeed.'

What was going on? Annabel didn't know, didn't care. She just wanted to be out of there, away from Rory Oakhurst who had broken her heart beyond repair. In two strides, Rory was at her side. He took the camera from her hands and placed it on a desk. Then he took hold of her arm and examined the inside of it carefully.

'I recognise these scratches,' he said. 'They're the same as the ones I get twice a year from cutting back the old hawthorn hedge that runs beside my cottage.'

Wondering if there was something she'd missed, Annabel tried to wrench herself free.

'Oh, Annabel, what am I going to do with you?' Rory asked in a totally different tone of voice. 'You're so sweet and so beautiful and so infuriatingly independent. Why didn't you tell me what was going on?'

Annabel stared at him in bewilderment.

'Zoe told me all about it, the whole thing, how Lawrence persuaded her she'd never get the breaks with me and that Sebastian was searching for an excuse to get rid of me — not true, incidentally. She told me that her reward for being instrumental in my downfall would be your job. How she swallowed that lot, I don't know. But you were right. She was even more

168

ambitious than I thought. So you followed me home, parked up the road somewhere and sat in my hawthorn hedge and took film on here.' He indicated the camera. 'Then you played drunk, a terrible performance, by the way, and slept on the floor at the foot of my bed. All to protect my reputation.'

It all sounded so silly. Annabel couldn't look at him.

'I didn't go that far. I slept on the sofa, actually.'

'But why on earth didn't you tell me?'

'Well, because I knew how much you liked Zoe and I didn't think you'd believe me,' she said in a small voice.

Rory took her face in his hands.

'Look at me, Annabel. I do like Zoe, and she's good at her job, but, Annabel, it's you I love. I love you. Are you listening?'

'Yes,' Annabel said, her heart beating wildly. 'Yes, I'm listening.'

'And now, although we've done this once already, in a wet carpark, if I remember correctly, unlike you, according to what you said at the time, I think there's every reason to do it again.'

Annabel gave up all pretence of coherent thought as Rory's mouth came down on hers. After all, it had started with a kiss . . .

THE END